C · O · N · C · E · R · T

C·O·N·C·E·R·T

K · O · N · Z · E · R · T

BY ELSE LASKER-SCHÜLER

Translated by Jean M. Snook

UNIVERSITY OF NEBRASKA PRESS

LINCOLN & LONDON

Library of Congress Cataloging
in Publication Data
Lasker-Schüler, Else, 1869-1945.
[Konzert. English]
Concert = Konzert / Else Lasker-
Schüler ;
translated by Jean M. Snook.
p. cm. –
(European women writers series)
ISBN 0-8032-2900-3 (alk. paper)
I. Title. II. Title: Konzert.
III. Series. PT 2623.A76K6613 1994
834'.912 – dc20 93-45427 CIP

Frontispiece: Else Lasker-Schüler
as Prince Jussef of Thebes,
c. 1910. Courtesy Kösel-Verlag
GmbH & Co.

CONTENTS

INTRODUCTION

Else Schüler was born on February 11, 1869, in Wuppertal-Elberfeld in the heavily industrialized Ruhr region of the province of North Rhine–Westfalia. She was the sixth and youngest child of Jewish businessman Aron Schüler and his wife Jeanette. They were a close family, with Else being particularly attached to her mother and her brother Paul. She attended school only until age eleven, when she contracted St. Vitus's dance, and was subsequently tutored at home. She enjoyed studying religion but does not seem to have applied herself in any other subjects. All that one teacher could say for her was that Else was basically "not all that stupid." Posterity, of course, has assessed her differently, as "the greatest poetess Germany ever had" (Gottfried Benn, lecture, 1952). By 1932, the year in which *Konzert* was published, she was well established as a poet, dramatist, and prose writer, as well as for her work in the visual arts, and she received the Kleist Prize for literature. She was also Jewish, and all too aware of the rampant growth of anti-Semitism in Germany, and of the serious threat posed by the increasing popularity of Hitler's National Socialist Party. The following year she was forced to flee the country, never to return.

Konzert was one of the last books published by a Jew in Germany. It is autobiographical, a collection of essays and vignettes that both entertain and engage the reader at a deeper level. Like Robert Schumann's piano suites, each in itself a perfect concert, Else Lasker-Schüler's work contains pieces that vary greatly in theme, mood, length, and complexity, yet they are unified by the medium and by the distinct and lyrical personality of the artist.

Lasker-Schüler's fame now rests mainly on her reputation as a poet, but she was also a performer. During her lifetime, in

Germany and in exile, she was much in demand for her dramatic readings, and knew well how to appeal to different audiences. This skill is manifestly evident in *Concert*. The scintillating prose style keeps the work attractive, while the frequent changes in topic keep it moving. Here is nourishment for both mind and soul. Proceeding in an apparently effortless and intuitive fashion, Lasker-Schüler is able to transform and transcend the everyday scenery and events that are her points of departure. She makes magical an unmagical corner of Germany, discerns the miraculous in the neglected and ignored, and finds wisdom and comfort in prayer and a cosmic perspective.

While professing to have no Weltanschauung, perhaps because she perceives the development of one as a tedious academic exercise, Lasker-Schüler clearly does have her own consistent view of the world, based on respect for plants, animals, and life itself. It may come as a surprise to some readers that *Concert* contains a warning about the climatic dangers of interfering "with the merry green leaf people who give us ozone and the breath of life." Lasker-Schüler was in some ways uncannily prophetic. Although relatively uneducated, she was nevertheless innately attuned to the world, and appreciated the worth of her own insights. In a delightful line in *Concert*, she calmly acknowledges that the scholar may need "thirty years of laborious studying to discover that which the poet mentions in passing."

Certainly art, for Lasker-Schüler, was something that came naturally in its own time. She began to draw when her letters "burst into bloom." And her son's natural talent was such that he seemed to "swim across the page." Actually, she felt that formal instruction impeded his progress. The creative process was a playful one. Words were like mussels "thrown up on the beach by waves and then collected by a poet in his little pail."

Most readers will be familiar with Lasker-Schüler's poetry in English translation. From remarks such as the above that are scattered throughout *Concert,* one can derive a sense of the poet's Weltanschauung and her *ars poetica,* of the innocence and purity of her approach to language. From the autobiographical material in *Concert,* one also gains a better sense of this astounding poet who "brought love into the world, that every heart might blossom blue."

To me, there is a sense of urgency about many of the personal anecdotes that makes them all the more poignant: the nostalgic memories of childhood, the humorous tales of her father, the encomia of companionship. It is as if Lasker-Schüler, already in her sixties and increasingly insecure in a politically hostile environment, is determined in these essays to hold fast the precious moments set in a Germany soon to be destroyed. For example, in the opening essay she was no doubt aware that her pilgrimage to her parents' graves was the last. She writes only, "When the great gate of the old Jewish cemetery closes behind me, another day has passed." Yet she imparts in these simple phrases a leaden sense of doors closing forever.

Like Virginia Woolf, Else Lasker-Schüler has an undercurrent in her prose that can move the reader rapidly into another dimension. For example, this twist comes at the end of the essay "The Train": "The big locomotives drive into all the cities, indeed, into all the countries of the world, but this one goes all the way to heaven."

The dark emotional tone set by such passages is certainly justified by the external events of Lasker-Schüler's life. As mentioned in *Concert,* her brother Paul died just before her thirteenth birthday. Her mother also died suddenly, when Else was twenty-one. She refers to both of them repeatedly in her works, yearning for the loving protection they provided, wishing in her more vulnerable moments to be "someone else's child." When she was twenty-four, she entered into an unhappy marriage with the physician Berthold Lasker, brother of the world chess champion Emanuel Lasker, and moved with him to Berlin. There she soon made contact with artistic circles, opened her own studio, left Lasker, and in 1899 gave birth to her only child, the son whom she named after her brother Paul.

By this time, Lasker-Schüler had completely broken with the establishment. She was living in penury but finding her own mode of self-expression and seeking her personal God. Although she frequently claimed to be lonely, Lasker-Schüler had a surprising number of close and significant friendships. The older Westfalian author Peter Hille, described with such love and respect in *Concert,* befriended her around the turn of the century, understood her inner nature, and encouraged her to write and publish poetry. For him, she took on a special identity that emphasized her inclination toward the exotic: she became Tino of Bagdad. A similar identity transformation occurred a decade later when she made friends with the Expressionist painter Franz Marc. This time she adopted a role modeled loosely on the biblical figure of Joseph, who had always fascinated her; she became Prince Jussuf of Thebes, alias The Malik. All three of these assumed names appear in or as the titles of major prose works, as yet untranslated, that precede *Concert.*

In the first three decades of this century, Lasker-Schüler lost all those whom she held dear. Peter Hille died in a train station in 1904. Her seven-year marriage to fellow writer and publisher Georg Levin, known more commonly by the name she gave him, Herwarth Walden, ended in 1910 when he left her for a younger woman he met in Norway. In November of 1913, Lasker-Schüler undertook to travel to Petersburg and

Moscow to help her friend Johannes Holzmann (whom she called Senna Hoy), but he was already fatally ill and died in prison. In March of 1914 she met the Austrian poet Georg Trakl, whose mellifluous poetic style was equaled only by her own; in November of the same year she responded to an urgent postcard from him, only to find that he had already committed suicide after the horrendous battle of Grodek. In 1915, as Lasker-Schüler had predicted, the war also claimed Franz Marc.

The greatest personal blow by far, though, came in 1927, when her beloved son Paul died of tuberculosis. Just as he is featured prominently in *Concert*, so too his mother's last prose work, *Das Hebräerland* (The Land of the Hebrews), published in exile ten years after his death, contains one of her most beautiful poems, to him:

> Again and again you will die on me
> In the parting year, my child –
>
> When the leaves flow away like tears
> And the twigs grow thin.

Through it all, she continued to write and to illustrate some of her own works. Not all her work was understood by her contemporaries, mainly because her early Expressionist style had a more tenuous connection to external reality than they might have wished. She and her husband even found it necessary to launch a lawsuit about one of her poems, "Leise sagen," which was reprinted without her permission and cited as evidence that she was "soft in the head."

There were successes, though. As mentioned in *Concert*, her first play, *Die Wupper* (*The Wupper*), was performed in Max Reinhardt's theater in Berlin. And *Concert* itself was greeted by one critic as a timeless mosaic of consolation and inspiration, a work whose melodious language remains with the reader long after the book has been finished (*Berliner Tageblatt*, No. 291, June 21, 1932).

Lasker-Schüler's flight from the Nazis in 1933 took her first to Switzerland. Entirely without means, she spent her first few nights there on a park bench. From Switzerland, she was able in the ensuing years to make three trips to Palestine, thus fulfilling a lifelong dream. However, she was elderly, did not speak the language, and had difficulty reconciling the Palestine she found with the Palestine she had envisaged. It was there that she died of heart failure in 1945, having published her famous final volume of poetry, *Mein blaues Klavier* (*My Blue Piano*), and having written a politically astute and prophetic play, *Ich und Ich* (*I and I*), that was suppressed by the executor of her estate until 1970 because it supposedly detracted from her "image."

We have Margarete Kupper to thank for her tireless efforts in cataloguing and bringing to light much of Lasker-Schüler's work, and for doing the groundwork for a forthcoming critical edition. In the last two decades, major and insightful scholarly works have been written on Lasker-Schüler, from Klaus Weissenberger's 1976 study of the mystical elements through Sigrid Bauschinger's excellent 1980 biography to Jakob Hessing's 1985 examination of her works from a predominantly Jewish standpoint.

The dtv (Deutscher Taschenbuch Verlag) nine-volume paperback edition of her complete works published in Germany in 1986 has brought Lasker-Schüler at last into the limelight she deserves, and the immense popularity of the edition confirms that her voice remains relevant to our own times.

Lasker-Schüler is a challenging writer to translate because of her highly figurative and idiosyncratic use of language. Much of the work is written in an almost dreamlike state, like an interior monologue. Abrupt transitions between past and present result in some awkward sections in the otherwise lyrical prose, sections that would have been smoothed out by a modern editor. I decided not to assume an editorial stance but to translate the original as accurately as I was able. The sections in Lasker-Schüler's native Westfalian dialect posed a particular problem. Clearly, there is no cross-cultural equivalent. Yet ideally the translation should indicate a change in pronunciation in these sections. In the attempt to remain true to the original to some extent, I analyzed whether the vowel sounds in the dialect had been raised or lowered from standard High German, and moved them in the same direction in English. For example, noting that the High German "ich" was rendered as "eck," "mich" as "meck," and "Die" as "de," I felt justified in dropping the English "I" down to "Ah." All footnotes are my own.

The translation of *Konzert* has been an absorbing and enjoyable undertaking. I hope that I have been able at least in part to convey the compelling character of the poetic persona. My thanks to Mrs. Elfi Boehm, who graciously entertained dozens of questions about dialect and idiom that were beyond the scope of dictionaries; to my husband Jim, whose careful critical reading of the entire manuscript yielded many improvements; and to the external referee for the University of Nebraska Press, Ruth Schwertfeger, whose own book on Else Lasker-Schüler recently appeared, and who provided me with good advice and many felicitous turns of phrase.

Jean M. Snook

C · O · N · C · E · R · T

We lived at the foot of the hill. It rose steeply up from our house into the forest. Anyone who had a bounding red heart could be up to the berry patch in five minutes. On Sundays whole families came climbing down the hill past our house. The children carried small baskets on their arms, filled to the brim, but their little blue-stained mouths showed what they had been picking to garnish the omelettes for their Sunday evening meal. I have always been so proud of our big forest. One had to look down into it, whether one wanted to or not, when climbing up Sadowa Street. At the foot of the street was my parents' home, outside the city, because our neighborhood only became the West End later on. There was always a fresh green breeze wafting out of the woods that fortified the lungs. And every tree, every bush that I come across today reminds me of our forest, into whose peaceful eyes I looked with laughter as a child. When the thunderstorms came from the four points of the compass, when the flashy black riders approached, my dear mama took a seat on the balcony, which seemed to hover freely in the air between east and west. So it seemed. As if one were sitting in small shallops between the waves of air; that induced my daring mother to get in. There were flashes of lightning from four clouds. Then over in the east, in the form of a prong, a burning dagger stabbed the heaving, excited, cloudy breast of heaven. My father recalled his venerable grandfather, the white-bearded Chief Rabbi of the Rhineland and of Westfalia. Shaken by the most awesome drama of the atmosphere, he would pray to Jehovah, making the sign of the stars as a Christian would of the cross. My father, however, was simply worried about his dahlias and pansies in the flowerbeds of our garden; and above all he feared for his ripening sour cherry tree and his miraculous bush. You see, it produced two types of fruit at the same time. My papa had introduced the gooseberry and the red currant to each other, had invited them both, and with the help of the gardener had married the two. Since then they had been growing harmoniously on one branch and stalk, and my father was very proud of this, rather like a statesman who had succeeded in uniting states. In any case, he considered what he had done to be just as important. But he was most moved by the magnificent weeping rose! It hung luxuriously over the newly embroidered delicate grass carpet, as if poured from a cornucopia. Many, many, many white roses (I didn't find them so sad at all in appearance) shimmered like a splendid train spread out in the glow of sunset. And last but not least the scaffolding of his new buildings rose up before my father's praying eyes. Still without stone or mortar, the buildings reminded me of a skeleton, on which the flesh and the agglutinant blood were missing.

After such a violent thunderstorm, workers always came running, bringing him the news that the upper story or the roof of one of his buildings had fallen onto the roof of a neighboring house – and there was no end to the lawsuits, to which the people of the city streamed as if to a comedy, and which always ended with a settlement. It was not uncommon for my father to bring the complainants home with him. Then the carousing began, and lasted through the night. Beginning in the late afternoon, we heard the litigants drinking to each other, doubling up with laughter after every toast, toasts my father could propose like no other person on earth, seasoning them with the spice of humor from the larder of his boisterous, generous heart. Early in the morning the guests from the trial relaxed in our lovely little garden. In my bed, I was awakened by the choralelike crescendo of my father's voice, which drowned out all other voices, and I knew that now he was showing the guests the crystalline pebbles that covered the path. Sometimes, even without the occasion of a storm, I heard my twelve-year-old papa with his snow-white hair pray to God for these stones, that they might not sink into the bowels of the earth. Even though I was still so small, it did move me in passing. On Sunday we often went for a drive in the vicinity of Elberfeld on the Ronsdorf Road; on either side magnificent, sunken forests, right and left valleys of unspeakable happiness, glowing darkly. We came upon traveling journeymen who sang as they walked. If they were very tired, my parents let them climb up on the driver's seat, requiring me to climb down. My beautiful sisters blossomed like flowers in pink and blue dresses, and my brothers, if they happened to be home from their boarding school in St. Goarhausen, marched along ahead of us with their friends, who always were in love with my sisters. I especially liked to wear little red calico dresses, and always had some hard candy that my mother had given to me hidden in one of my pockets. I loved my mama ardently, she was my friend, my idol, my strength, my absolution, my emperor.

Napoleon Bonaparte must certainly have looked like her, and that explains why she had a Napoleon collection. My papa was one of the boys, with whom I played cops and robbers. And he always reasserted his authority by buying me a bag of candy after the storm of a battle. We went together to the circus, but woe was me if I took too long getting dressed and we arrived at the last moment and then I had to go to the bathroom just "one more time" and we missed the first act. Then he grumbled throughout the entire performance and cursed me.

As a boy he had been roundly thrashed by his parents for his cursing. However, the farmers of Westfalia, where he was born the fourth son of twenty-three children, loved him for

3

his cursing. When he was three years old he was already jumping over the animal hedges and playing all the pranks that are expected of boys. My father had a particular soft spot for the theater in Elberfeld. If he wasn't bringing actors home to dinner, it was stunt riders. Then we had to have magic tricks, one, two, three more rounds, and he always managed to put a surprise cracker in August von Renz's napkin. My dear father, my beloved mother, in the strange, dark, working-class city with the thousands of smokestacks over the Wupper Valley in the Rhineland! Lonely now, I wander through the charming narrow streets, climb the many hills, and come suddenly to the bottom of a long flight of stairs. Arriving at the top, I look into a garden full of violets and wonderful lilac lawns of lady's-smock. Many tenants now live in the house where I grew up, but when the sunset is mirrored in its windows, like the rubies of heaven, it seems to me that the Angel Gabriel stands sentinel over it alone. That comforts me. I place my mother's favorite flowers, mignonettes, on her grave, and bring violets for my father, and under the broken pillar sleeps the youngest of my brothers, a saint, beautiful as Apollo – he died with a pure heart. Near my parents' graves, my little girlfriend Hanni is buried. I inherited her doll: Inge-borg. It had blue eyes as she did and wore a necklace around its neck as she did. When the great gate of the old Jewish cemetery closes behind me, another day has passed. Late sun-shine accompanies me cautiously down the many steps right into the center of the lively city of Elberfeld.

OUR LITTLE GARDEN

To my beloved little Paul

At the time my father was having the paths covered with glittering gravel, whose crystal both of us admired from the bower, I was still not properly aware of the little garden. It was, in fact, a living toy store with trees of all colors of green and bushes draped with blossoms that shaded the many colorful flowers, the primroses, the forget-me-nots, velvet pansies, asters, and dahlias. Today I would like to place the entire little garden in a terrarium on my table. In the fall, the wild chestnuts in their prickly shells fell on the gravel that was already crushed underfoot and mixed with earth; some also fell into the tufted, worn-out grass with a plop! We children kept the green hedgehogs, as we called the enchanting things, and brought them to the round iron table on which we set out our wares for sale, my four friends and I. And we collected the large leaves, already rusted by rain, ribbed them or bound them into cabbages for sale at our stand. We also went to work on the bushes, little thieves that we were, because the milky toy torpedoes were in great demand. Carefully, I placed one after the other in the boys' hands. Only *I* was allowed to pick them and was responsible for the number. Pülle Kaufmann, however, secretly – as he assured me, unintentionally – now and then let a particularly fat one fall to earth and squashed it with his heel. Then my friends flew into a rage, tramped on the late flower beds, and tumbled head over heels into the thorns of the rose bushes. Covered with scratch wounds, thorn splinters in our fingers, each of us ran bawling to our mamas; only to meet again very soon at the entrance to the garden with consoled little chocolate mouths. Pülle, indeed, had a currant stuck in the groove of his round chin. Our little garden had become our common playroom, but only in the fall, because in the spring "Mrs. Schüler" drank coffee under the silver ash tree with her daughters. My five-year-old friends had great respect for my mama, who could not be compared to other mamas. Also, she spoke French to my older sisters, especially when we children were not supposed to know

5

something, usually when there was a pleasant surprise for us. Only in their Sunday suits, with a message from home, did my playmates shyly dare to approach my smiling, majestic mama. She treated them with the degree of attentiveness appropriate for young gentlemen. After a while they departed in civilized fashion, bowing deeply and politely before pushing proudly through the garden gate, and taking with them a piece of cake covered with fruit. Between the lobed, hairy ears of the leaves, the hazelnuts were finally getting ripe! Only Alfred Baumann and I knew about them. I trusted him, he was already seven years old and wore his hair parted at the side, not scratched up on end like the bristles of a toothbrush. And his wonderful checkered tie matched my dress exactly. He was my bridegroom – and would not permit the other boys to poke me in the ribs. He regularly climbed back over the fence after Paul Stern and the other Pülle and the learned Walter, who already wore glasses, had run home. With his large new front teeth he could crack open the nuts in no time – they made such cracking sounds – and we peered around like busy squirrels. He always gave me the first kernel to bite. He was a gentleman, even if he did crack two nuts in a row for himself right afterwards and simply spit the shells back into the bushes. A single one of the secret nuts tasted better to us than a whole bag bought at the market. Sometimes we also found gooseberries and red currants together on one bush, the bush that my father, with the help of the gardener, had married. A little natural drama. Strictly forbidden fruit, because my sisters picked them for the cook to go with the roast. But there was still a luscious red cherry on our sour cherry tree, up at the top, high in the branches. The tree blossomed in May like rosy snow over the balcony of our tower. We were planning, Alfred Baumann and I, ... when suddenly a great tit flew past us and discovered the welcome food. It sat on the bare branch up in the faded crown, puffed itself up, laughingly opened its feathered belly and ate the cherry right before our noses.

THE TRAIN

Up in the garret, as the people in Wuppertal call their attics, was my youngest brother's laboratory, "the poison room," in which he had vials with different salts and acids and all sorts of the strangest-colored chemicals. It was the verdigris-yellow sulphur cube that I found particularly fascinating. My brother was most interested in chemistry and natural sciences, but he also greatly enjoyed building small locomotives. One could hear their whistles blowing all the way down at the bottom of the stairs. Sometimes he called me into his laboratory when the tiny steam-engine was racing along the tracks at top speed, its little wheels spinning like those of an express-train locomotive. Around the table it went, and through the little St. Gotthard Pass, which my brother had built and tunneled through. I was allowed to put my two dainty wax doll twins, both were called Meta, into the first-class car, specially attached for them. I was only inexplicably afraid of the flasks . . . in the blue one . . . sat a ghost. . . . When my brother opened one or the other of them, the air smelled so poisonous I thought I would choke. But he was a magician, because from green and yellow he could conjure blue and back again. Two acids that he poured together suddenly became lilac, and a drop of saltpeter was enough to change the lilac to red. On the shelves in the corner lay a pile of Greek and Latin books and a huge old Bible with a weathered white leather cover. My brother was devout. But I was interested in his herbaria with the delicate quaking grasses and carefully dried flowers, bindweeds, sweet peas, white thorn, and a large mullein. In the glass cupboard was his coin collection, some were already rusted, and his splendid stone collection. I was fascinated by the large lapis lazuli and by the crystal – still embedded in the rock. When evening came, my brother did his homework. He was in the highest grade in high school and tutored me, because I dreamed too much in school. I could add and multiply halfway to one hundred; in geography I knew only the cities and rivers where I had already been, or the sea, in which I had splashed about. My brother, however, had divine patience, and at the end he always told me my favorite story again, of Joseph and his brothers, and he showed me the picture of how Joseph was sold. One day in the winter, on a Sunday, my brother died. Exactly as he had said to our beloved mother – on a Sunday. A halo lay around his sunny hair – he smiled, he had been pure of heart and saw the dear God. I wore a crepe band around my arm and a long necklace with black glass beads around my neck. The children at school secretly envied me because of this, and I thought myself so grown up. But once at daybreak, when I was still asleep, my dead brother stood before my little bed and took me by the hand. We climbed up to the garret, into the poison room, and there he poured alcohol into the tank of the locomotive, exactly like a stoker; then it raced around the tracks just so – and he said to me: "The big locomotives drive into all the cities, indeed, into all the countries of the world, but this one goes all the way to heaven."

THE SQUIRRELS

My youngest brother Paul loved going through the woods with me. He knew every tree and every bush by name; he knew how to carefully bend back the thorniest branches, when a rose looked at him. As a matter of principle, he never picked a flower from life, never broke a branch in bloom from its stalk, nor willfully removed a plant from its spot in the sun or refreshing shade. "Mercy begins with the protection of plants!" he often said to me. He would rather leave behind some strands of his ash-blond hair than carelessly snap the young thorn stalks off the summer bushes. My brother was a young king, a monk, the sky his blue cathedral. Out of it he came down to earth every morning, and I was very proud that he walked hand in hand with me through the woods. When the two of us discovered a walnut tree, and there happened to be a bench close by, my brother lifted me onto the seat beside him, and we listened for the approach of the squirrels, who didn't keep us waiting too long. But even if we did not discover a place to sit, he placed me somewhere; best of all I liked to sit high up on his shoulder, because my dead brother had grown very tall, and I crept along beside him like a little beetle over the fragrant, acrid forest floor. I was so fond of the walnut trees because of their thick shells that surrounded the hard kernel; the little split things served as the weigh-scales for me and my playmates, when we played storekeepers; and I was very grateful to the squirrels for fetching nuts from the tree just as we watched them, nibbling them very carefully out of their case, and throwing the two unpalatable halves neatly down into my tucked-up little skirt. The same squirrel always came. It had a chocolate-colored tail, and I clapped my hands when I saw it, because it used its tail to sweep the forest clean. Suddenly it would be there, sitting in the crown of a tall walnut tree, and cracking open a fat nut for itself, making a zigzag sound through the quiet forest. The birds, of course, continued singing undisturbed, bright and dark green songs, and sometimes the cuckoo sang: it preferred to sit in the copper beech. Then my brother counted: cuckoo, cuckoo, cuckoo, cuckoo, cuckoo, cuckoo, cuckoo, seven times – that's exactly how old I was.

I trust my literary instincts and do not question why again and again I feel compelled to write a composition about the plants of our world. This morning I eavesdropped on a lively conversation that the trees were having with each other in front of my window. That led me to conclude that plants, like people and animals, are personally aware of blood relationships. Because the portly linden tree, with great concern, reminded the small, thin linden tree to stand up straight: "Stand up straight!" That kind of interest is only shown by a mother for her child. I already noticed several times in a veiled way, still in the mist of my senses, how the arm branches of the mother linden anxiously bent down to the daughter, and I heard the mother tree, with its luxuriant foliage, audibly admonish the daughter; and I too must admit with regret that the trunk of the young linden is indeed inclined to grow crooked. In contrast, the tanned bodies of the chestnut and elder trees stretch straight up every day as soon as the earth becomes light! The mother linden observed them with understandable envy. Both friends were the same age as her daughter, whose dreaminess was enough to make her leaves turn yellow!! But even when the daughter was still bound to the umbilical root, pushing her way in the soil, she was already longing in her most delicate germ to grow into the supreme happiness of heaven. And thus it came about that her life took place only in the innermost heart of her pith, unconcerned about all the external influences that threatened to hamper her physical growth. Trees – indeed all plants – possess a heart that really beats, that drives the blood through their cells, through even the smallest of their leaves. Fruits are able to turn red, and especially with the cherry, love brings the blood into its cheeks. Plants have real hearts, some of which bleed devoutly in the morning, as is the case with the young linden tree. I love that tree like a favorite companion, which actually does not belong in this story "The Trees by Themselves." But I take a personal interest in the fate of this delicate and dreamy tree. From much, much pondering and worrying and humility, the gentle saint is neglecting her figure. And yet, I noticed a silvery light around her "arborescence" in the twilight, a ray emanating from the pure soul of the chosen one, whose spark rises up to God. I knew it, she had once seen an angel, who blessed her. Her leaves always rustle ardently, even when the threatening west invades the June stillness with thunder and lightning. The other trees, though, hardly seem to notice a difference in the air, at least they do not allow themselves to be disturbed from their game of counting the seven days of Creation; to be named in all kinds of intonations: their daily pastime. Like a swarm of butterflies, Monday and Tuesday, Wednesday, green Thursday, shimmering Friday and Saturday and quiet Sunday hover over the laughing, childlike trees. They are content with the beauty of the ground, in which they stand secure and are fulfilled; they chat with the tilled garden plot and the pansies and forget-me-nots, blue and pink, in its flowerbeds. When the nanny goat next door bleats, the trees and all the flowers and grasses rejoice. Even the primal leaf parents in paradise were amused by the hearty bleating of billy goats. Dear God in his youth would tease them with a long, long quaking grass that dropped down so quickly out of the clouds. The cackling of the hens, though, was ignored even by Adam and Eve, and it does make the mother linden nervous. Then she breathes impatiently, ends the game early, and explains in a pleasant-sounding voice: "Sunday!" And there is not a bird who would have uttered one more peep. A game of light entertainment that has been played since the beginning of the world, the counting of the

11

seven days of Creation; colorful in the air, strong on the earth, bright over the water, and fair under the sky, it lives on only in the sleight of branch of the trees. And they actually know nothing of "time," they do not wear a watch tucked in the fibrous crevice of their back. Instead, they let eternity tick under their trunks. When the Good Lord strews new stars over the carpet of heaven and his eternal hand playfully wipes out a number of them, then a comet arises with a gold-speckled peacock's train. The wonderful trumpet of the east heralds the early announcement of his coming, first of all to the trees of the plant kingdom. It begins to storm tempestuously in the treetops: the Messiah is coming, to gladden their hearts with his beauty! And suddenly they all join together, forming a green congregation; indeed, they even uproot themselves, rejoicing in their good fortune; we humans just don't notice it, because their keen expectation of the magnificent star keeps them rooted to the spot. I understand the world more every day; just like the tree, like the flower and all plants understood it ever since the first seed was sown. Who knows a tree that is a philosopher, or a pine that would construct a *Weltanschauung* from its wood? Why would the tree or even the rose need a *Weltanschauung,* or comprehensive worldview? They most solemnly allow themselves to be viewed by the world, which observes them proudly and leisurely as its children's blooming inheritance of pleasure. They shouldn't even think of rummaging in God's monumental cupboard! And yet quite a few people attempt to unlock it, often, in fact, to break it open! They get their fingers squeezed or reach into emptiness, even if they do, now and then, get hold of a tiny handkerchief for their wisdom. That which is a high priority for us is a low priority there, and that which is a sparkling high priority for God is a dull low priority for us. The unassuming self-restraint of the plants puts me to shame, even if, God

12

knows, I have never allowed myself to construct a *Weltan-schauung* (due in part, perhaps, to laziness). That just goes too far for me. The way to me amounts to only a leap for the world, a short ride on the subway; for me to go to the world is a voyage to the stars. But once the world did pick me up from the scene, to wit, we went to school together; the world always did my homework for me and helped me in religion. We went hand in hand in a circle, always in a circle! World is in world as man is in man, animal in animal and tree in leaf and vice versa leaf again in tree and everything in everything and all in all and All in God. Amen. The plants know that, every one of them, and the *dreamy* tree is inspired by one wish, ... *to grow up into heaven*. In her eagerness for the highest holy praise, such a God-filled linden tree forgets to stand up straight! I think I would like to be a tree, if only because sometimes a bird comes and sings in my branches.

THE HEART OF THE PLANTS

Someone I Do Not Know Wrote This about Me:

Else Lasker-Schüler, this infinitely small, infinitely large star in an infinitely large, infinitely small world of literature, dreams of "Trees by Themselves." And tells us: "Trees, indeed all plants, possess a heart that really beats, that drives the blood through their cells, through even the smallest of their leaves. Fruits are able to turn red, and especially with the cherry, love brings the blood into its cheeks. Plants have real hearts, some of which bleed devoutly in the morning, as is the case with the young linden tree." One can hardly assume that the poet follows the conference proceedings of English natu-ralists. And one can assume even less that she derives her inspiration from them. And yet it is known that just a few weeks ago, at the naturalists' conference, the Indian scholar Bose presented his sensational discovery of the heart of plants. Using ingenious, complicated control systems, he was able to furnish proof of plants' blood circulation and cardiac activity, even of the sounds of the heart. – Bose, the Indian mystic and scholar, needed thirty years of laborious studying to discover that which the poet mentions in passing. No one notices this. Although it is fundamentally one of the most amazing proofs of the extent to which what the true artist "sees" approaches the "objective truth." Of how beauty and truth in the higher sense are one and the same. And we can feel particularly happy that this proof that the creative, artistic imagination "is right" comes in our days, in a time in which, as a rule, only adding machines and their human appendages are right.   R.

FRIENDSHIP AND LOVE

When one no longer has a mother, in whose love heaven and earth are transfigured, one longs with all one's heart for a good friend, male or female. One knows, though, "if one is a friend to oneself," with whom one is dealing! If one practices loyalty to oneself, one is seldom disappointed; even if one cannot forgive oneself certain stupidities. Even though my stupid remarks far surpass in value my clever remarks. I am even proud of my stupid remarks: "One soul and – not a single thought, one heart and one beehive."* Being with yourself does get a bit boring after a while, but who would not put up with "oneself"? Yet the fulfillment of all longing for friendship means encountering one's second face. A friend is always nec-

*These are witty alterations of the well-known German sayings: "Two minds with but a single thought," and "one heart and one soul," meaning, to be the best of friends.

essary for one to see one's image in the friend, as the lover sees his completion in the beloved. Do you still remember when your school-friend didn't show any interest in playing your game in the schoolyard? It was not without reason that one was annoyed with the "spoilsport"! In life, one makes friends often, even – "eternal" friends, and I also don't believe in the once-in-a-lifetime love that poets sing of. To be sure, each newly dawning love has its own color, but the devotion and ecstasy are always the same. Every time I met Señor Paolo, the Mexican consul, on the Lago Maggiore, my admiring eyes would close, blinded by his olive-golden aura. That is how I also once loved a "sky-blue" person. I also know a sacred poet who stands in the middle of my room on the place where the carpet belongs: a purple lilac bush. Is it not true that musical notes often are or appear to be pink, brown and darkened silver, or orange-colored? How is that to be explained? I know one thing, one should provide love with accommodations fit for a king, and friendship with accommodations fit for an Indian. Every love, every friendship that endures serves as a model to the world. Love, above all, because it is not of this world, its abiding here does not lie within our power. However, we are still able to fan the flame of friendship. Like a storm bride, love approaches from love-west or like the rustling of palms from the far East. It is a comet filled with promises, if one stands embraced by it, entirely in light. A shooting star, surprising, love dives down invisibly into the heart, which has been enchanted and deprived of a will of its own. A shooting heaven! The drop of a burst heaven sweetens our blood and colors our heart blue. Love is a state into which one is transported by divine events. A state before or after death: an atmosphere that sinks into one's heart and makes one happy. An angel, of two gazes melted in each other. Friendship, however, is of this world. We are able to deal with it; it lies in our power to let it blossom or wilt, glow or grow cold. Its duration is determined by the measure of mutual trust. Love, on the other hand, is cared for on the other side of time. Any effort to hinder it or attract it on one's own authority is in vain! Love is a state consecrated by the highest of the high, one should allow it to come over one like fragrance. One should not manipulate love. . . . I advise friends, however, to take complete control of their friendship, it can be dealt with, as one says! Friendship can be won, friends are able to consolidate their friendship through proof of mutual loyalty. A long-standing proverb says, as well: "Little presents keep a friend-ship alive." But love cannot be bought, not even with the ruby of the heart. And I despise the cavalier who – when it is a matter of the success of pure love – thinks he can conquer the lady's heart with jewels. The loving man or woman longs to possess the soul of the other embodied in the loveliest frame. For the camellia over the Señor's heart I would have given half my life. And it is no arbitrary remark that "marriages are made in heaven." That is only true, though, of the marriages that are brought from heaven to earth! Two eyes kissing each other bring the angel of love to the world, bring the blissful state over two hearts. How, though, does one explain a one-sided, so-called "unrequited" love? A love that is not recipro-cated. Is the great event thwarted by an accident, a divine one, naturally? Certainly in countless cases things on earth remain incomplete. Does perhaps a counterforce interrupt the en-chanting stream of love from chosen one to chosen one? Did the angel of love break his wings, or who put a damper on the happiness before it reached its completion? Not infrequently, the messenger of love likes to play a trick on both the lovers. The Greeks called their little god of love Cupid, personifying the marksman who aims at the heart. We don't even try any-more these days to explain to ourselves and to understand the

16

unembodied rogue. And yet sometimes one has him to thank for a so-called hit. How else does it come about that one sometimes loves several people at the same time? It is not so easy to die a "natural death" of mass love, nor to attain bliss. Just as so many lovers break their hearts over love, friends are wont to break their heads thinking about the problem of their friendship. They practice standing by each other in danger, and play skillfully with words in the game of conversation. They seek to be alike not only in their actions, but also again and again in their wishes, true Indians, to a copper hair, to a black hair, but when it comes to the point they confess to the same color: The blue jaguar! The blond tiger! The friend perceives his friend in the frame of unity, lovers look at each other mutually in the mirror of the brook. – Love, which no overture precedes, does not take a bow. Yet it highly respects what happens when two people, overcome by the power of their emotions, sink into each other's arms. Is there anything else as elemental? And in the simplest form? Who looks in other people's windows nowadays when going for a walk? I have never been able to break the habit, but – nobody sits at the window. I more often see cat burglars! Friendship is strengthened by common danger and by the play of two friends, but there is no endeavor that can reduce or increase the degree of love by an iota. Besides, in these times there is no time for overtures or prologues to love. Basically, what does love have to do with getting ahead; daydreaming is a thing of the past! Even if it were a great friendship, with friends who mutually support each other. And I can't keep from speaking of love, if it is ardent, in whatever way, hear ye!! then it crowns the world. One should be aware of the miraculous flower – once it has blossomed at the edge or in the middle of the heart, its perfume overpowers everyday life and devalues all our other affections. Love creates its vitality from itself, as the star its light, the sun its warmth. It is precisely this great purity and unity that elevate real love above every other feeling. It does not go out hunting for attractions. One is frequently surprised how this person, of all people, can love that one? And vice versa. Love is a shooting heaven, a little piece of burst heaven that falls unexpectedly into the heart of two and exudes a state of great rejoicing. Terrible crises, however, are left behind by love's decay. When love has gone out of someone's life, his heart engulfs his head. Yesterday he still thought himself the true Croesus of this world, and the bankruptcy of love hits him hard. The woman, whom one loved infinitely and worshiped to the skies above with eyes of the redeemed, freed from earth's gravity, now suddenly presents herself in her mortality! Such blows of love are like operations that leave big scars. It is entirely different when the bond of love loosens as intended by a higher will, when it decomposes organically like beds of flowers that bid farewell to summer; they celebrate a loving parting from the lost heart of the summer day. There is never cause for the cooling of love. All the reasons that are brought forward are excuses. Love simply doesn't moralize. Lovers transform vice into virtue. Left bare by love, who installed herself as a queen – who are you now and who is he in his everyday fog who just recently lit up the sky like lightning? Friendship, however, can be restored. Two friends who have lost touch and find each other again build iron bridges over the gap in their friendship. Differences of opinion that did not cause moodiness strengthen the backbone of friendship. Moodiness is friendship's lukewarm vice, generosity is the alliance's virtue. Friends do get tired of each other, as the saying goes! If they find no common interests to talk about. Lovers, on the other hand, have the moon and stars fall into their lap and say nothing. . . . Love flourishes best under the bud of the unspoken word. Friends have to communicate more audibly and long to become more alike every day. Lovers less alike; mutual admiration; the law of love! Lovers should take it to heart. To create new perspectives again and again! To expand the space again for the wings of love. I sat silently for hours with the "blue wonderperson" – at the well "before the archway"* – and our two loving hearts were fused together in marriage.

> I would like to be silent forever
> Through life and death,
> Like a song still unplayed
> In the strings of the violins.
> I love the blue flowers
> In the tall quaking grass
> And your blue soul
> Under blue glass.

But to my friend, who is used to my steady chatter, I write something similar in the following version:

> I would like to talk with you
> From evening to morning.
> Come! everything is as it was again;
> Dull as dishwater.
> I love the sea, the wet one,
> In its fourposter bed,
> And if you aren't flush with money
> I'll get you the ticket "on tick."

Also, for your friendship – to put it to the test – I prescribe a trip together. What one does not find out in life at the usual

*"At the well before the archway" is the opening line of the fifth song in Schubert's famous song-cycle "Winterreise" or winter journey, composed to poetry by the lesser-known poet Wilhelm Müller. In the original German, Lasker-Schüler's two poems that follow are structural emulations with phonetic echoes, and could well be sung to the Schubert melody.

pace often comes to light when going by train, with the world unbound and hurtling past. Or – the great flight is a success! Both come home bonded by travel. – Lasting friendships, seldom the deepest, stem from childhood years. Turned golden in memory, various events hammer together two children who have grown up. The effects of different types of milieux and lifestyles are not able to separate childhood friends, on the contrary, in the more mature person friendship changes into fraternal love toward his playmate. By way of contrast, it often happens that two people who loved each other ardently will not understand each other when they meet years later. In their memory, the love means only an "affair" they got over. We, though, we who recognized love as paradise, feel that even its darkness – when love dies – divinely unites us. Everyone experiences the eclipse of love in his heart at some time in his life. That one doesn't die as a result of it is something I still don't understand. Obsessed with love just a minute ago, and already forgotten by it for no reason at all! Eyes that were home to me close themselves forever. The leaden morning of apathy rises ruthlessly over my life. We separated, because it became cool in our hearts and dark. . . . This reason alone accounts for a natural separation. That's why a marriage based on love, whether blooming wild or fenced in, is the only actually reasonable type of marriage. Who is still able to love with the love as it falls from heaven? And who can still be a friend to the friend?

SPITZ DOGS

The First Spitz: Rogue

Many people have their hobbyhorse, I have my spitz. They are by far the smartest dogs of the dog species, and I can tell tales about them. Our neighbor's spitz barked furiously when a beggar approached his garden gate, bringing all the people out into the street. Until his master himself came out of the house, out of whose uppermost window my girlfriend's upper body protruded, until her bright eyes discovered me in front of the hedge that separated our gardens. In no time we were standing beside each other; my little bosom friend's red-haired brother Fritz and the Rogue came and joined us. Rogue was the spitz's name. And he was already sniffing around in my pockets where I kept the sugar cubes for him. His loud barking made me nervous. He knew that, and without any reason at all he would leap at me making a deafening noise. He just happened to be an intelligent spitz, and when the little brother and sister came without him, I missed him. He had long silver-gray hair the color of his master's, of old Mr. Springmayer's, who informed us children again and again, as he observed his dog with restrained emotion, that it was an expensive, pedigree breed! Finally, his fixed, icy eyes would melt, and Friedrich, who was a bad boy, tickled us girls secretly on the nape of the neck. That was probably also the reason that Mr. Springmayer bought nothing but the most expensive collar for his barking treasure; it was made of red morocco leather and decorated with bells! That's what Rogue wore. And the little bells accompanied his clever barking. The dog belonged to the Springmayer family; simply "Spring-mayer's spitz." In the summer he was clipped, right on his birthday, the 17th of August, and I will never forget the mem-orable day, not in my entire life – when on the spitz's fifth birthday father Springmayer, who was prevented from com-ing because of a flare-up of his permanent cold, entrusted the clipping of his darling to his son Friedrich. With a searching look, he also sent us off, the two girlfriends, who volunteered to accompany Fritz. We set off cheerfully with father Spring-mayer's dog to have it clipped according to exact instructions.

It so happened that the high-spirited young dog hairdresser got deadly serious about it and instead of just trimming the dog's hindquarters, as he was supposed to, he gave it a radical shave, taking off the entire coat. We were absorbed in looking at the instruments and bottles and all sorts of things behind glass, and did not notice the atrocity until it had already been committed. Horrified, we spinelessly led the violated spitz stark naked through the city streets. In front of the window display of a butcher shop our Rogue made an energetic stop; not so much on account of the sausages as of the clear polished window, in which he was mirrored with big eyes. He, who seemed to feel good after the clip, was seized by an unprecedented panic. Just as we had sunk our heads when we saw him, he let his tail droop, looked at each of us silently with an accusing gaze, sniffed the shiny glass, yapped reproachfully at me and at Fritz's sister, leaped up, whining, at Fritz, and refused to follow us any farther. He knew his master as well as we did, and the old man would not have given up his spitz for all his brats, as kids are called along the Wupper River, especially since he had retired and no longer needed the children for family photographs. His photography studio in the eastern part of the garden had been inhabited since then by cacti, purified, as if in a glass mission house. In the morning he used to go out to the heathen plants with his Bible to read them the story of Creation. While that was going on, Fritz smoked tobacco from his edified father's long pipe, comfortably sprawled in the colorfully embroidered easy-chair. We children at the same time remembered the spiny pugs and green snakes he kept in earthenware pots – and how he loved the spitz first and foremost!! His strict father was the only person in the world whom Fritz feared; his learned school principal was a sheep compared with his stern papa. White as chalk, his knees knocking, he carried the animal in his trembling arms.

"I'm going to jump into the Wupper for cover!" His sister held on to the spitz's right paw, I his left. Suddenly the dog got out of our hands, leaped over Fritz's shoulder right onto the back of a female bulldog who, probably believing herself threatened with a sex murder, bit our beloved Rogue in his exposed throat, so violently that he perished – our dear, dear spitz! – but we the bereaved were saved. With the corners of our mouths looking mischievous but with heavy hearts we began the funeral procession – homewards. As though he sensed it, in spite of an approaching storm, old Mr. Springmayer waited for us, sneezing, in front of his garden gate, and we began to declaim to the horrified man in tearful chorus the ballad that Fritz had made up on the way and rehearsed with us, which father Springmayer resignedly accepted. Indeed he even attempted to console us sobbing children if possible and praised our presence of mind for having carried the wounded spitz to the vet, who removed the hair from the dog's upper body as well as the already shorn hindquarters, in order to be able to treat the wound more easily. But while the vet was working on him, the dear, dear Rogue died. . . . In the afternoon, we children met at the Bull's Basin, a place close by to go for an outing, past young bulls and delicious blueberries in the forest in whose valley our houses were located. We giggled confidentially until Fritz threatened to beat us black-and-blue if we should ever tell his father on him. Then he broke a branch off the rose bush, cleaned it with his pocketknife and bent it into a cross. On the evening of the same day my little friends called on me to come to the burial. Old Mr. Springmayer was busily digging the spitz's grave with his big shovel. Now and then a tear crept over his eyelids and down his wrinkled cheek; every time this happened he took his glasses off and wiped them clear again with his dotted red handkerchief. We nudged each other and had a hard time not to burst out laughing. The old man cast a stern gaze at his son, but Friedrich took his little cross and turned his brown eyes up to heaven. At the same time his sister folded her hands and said her evening prayer: "I am small, my heart is pure, and no one will live in it except for the spitz." . . . And I, deeply moved, picked a few forget-me-nots out of the grass, blue ones and pink ones, and laid them shyly on Rogue's grave. Father Springmayer, however, had carved a plaque out of the lid of a cigar box, on which he had painted in indelible jet black: "Here lies my loyal watchdog Rogue in peace."

The Second Spitz: Oscar

. . . whose acquaintance I made in a small booth set up by a traveling entertainer in the arcade in the center of Berlin. At that time I didn't yet know what I should do for the rest of the day and spent the entire morning behind the wooden door pasted with posters. Watched the colorful hustle and bustle of the humming chansonniers, stood in as the magician's helper; Berlin had made quite an impression on him. Soon I understood as well as the sorcerer with his black elderberry beard how to conjure up mysterious Barbary doves out of the magic eggs. In addition, I arranged the glittering little bouquets of dainty colored feathers and artificial flowers on a large tray. At the end of the performance, the magician elegantly brought them forth out of a handkerchief and threw them to the ladies in the parquet. I was actually seriously interested only in the spitz, who wore a hat made of playing cards. He was a 66 artist, a card champion. No one from the audience had ever succeeded in winning a game against him. His girlfriend Grete, a coquettish but devoted poodle, leaped through hoops and danced on a silver ball in front of the audience, but she also tried to make her boyfriend's life easier; Oscar was ambitious, as no other spitz before him who had ever stood on the stage, and he would have liked best to simply spring at the throat of that clown or that exaggerated female act. All this was prevented by the poodle-lady, even if she did now and then use her curly silk paw to pull back the curtain so that the spitz could check on what was going on. The curtain separated the artists' room and makeshift lavatory from the auditorium. The Viennese Girl, in particular, got on the spitz's nerves. Every evening, whether she got applause or not, she was prepared to sing an extra little song. The spitz by this time already knew her rendition of the fairy tale of the stork by heart, complete with silly trills. It insulted him, especially since he had grown up with storks and claimed to know from experience that the stork had no particular interest in contributing to the increase of the human race. Now I was in love with Oscar, had him tell me the story of his life again and again. The spitz was born in a small city in the Mark Brandenburg, in August as well, like Rogue of my first story. And indeed, at the same time as two storks, who immediately started clacking for worms in their nest on the roof of a sturdy farmhouse. Finally it was time for the spitz's act: Professor Oscar, the first master 66 player in the world. Great curiosity in the audience and noise. He, however, with perfect training, stepped onto the stage, which stands for the world. I will try to give a cool and factual account of the following event. It is important to me to show the readers, to impart to the readers, the consciousness of animals. Instinct is not the last word on the matter, Ladies and Gentlemen. Attention! – Professor Oscar leaps up on the raised chair in front of his little card-table. It has long legs painted yellow, and the public can look right through it. Thus, each member of the audience can determine for himself: neither the director nor anyone else from the troupe has a hand in the game. I too, since I know how to play 66, came forward to play with the maestro. The spitz surveyed the audience searchingly; I sat at his right side, both of us under strict observation by the crowd. I shuffled the cards, placed my partner's openly before him on the table; I held mine in my hand, otherwise it was exactly as I would have played with a two-handed creature. Professor Oscar was, accordingly, at a disadvantage, and yet a card game developed such as happens in the rarest cases between two first-class players. I actually forgot that I was sitting across from a dog and began to make an effort, thought I had lured him into the trap with my next-to-last ten of spades, but the master tapped with his black paw excitedly on his king of spades, which I placed on top of my card for him. It had come to the crunch now, and how the spitz's forehead wrinkled from concentration, his intelligent eyes sank back into their sockets as he considered his next move. He calculated, watching me cunningly, until his last card, the queen of hearts, beat my knave of hearts. That was the third game of 66 that my partner had won in the same evening performance. With his head stretched back, he awaited the sugar laurel. Soon all the Berliners came to play 66 with the spitz. The little theater of boards and beaded curtains became the court variety show. In the mornings, I was allowed to take care of the spitz and the poodle-lady. The dogs were entirely entrusted to me while the director and the actors sat in the Pirate's Cellar and drank away the evening's proceeds.

CONCERT

I heard the trees rustling with orchestral accompaniment from the ocean; it was September, and the day lay down with me earlier, eager for the concert. The autumn storm blew a new autumn song in the leafy bagpipes of the chestnut trees, and early in the morning the childlike cloud formations danced over the back of the world. Then the little sun came in a play dress with golden dots. Each time she shines on the earth, she thinks of it as playing with the big earth ball!! Oh, there had been so much dull weather during the summer, but now at last she held the neglected earth again in the playful rays of her hands. We who were sitting together, tired of the year, suddenly weren't freezing anymore and thought: Just look at what that golden child can do! I have often heard it screaming heatedly behind the door of its heavenly playroom for its dark friend, the earth. Nobody believes me when I say that. But all weather reports run aground on the rock of revelation. Only the frog came into the world with that talent. His prognosis about the weather is correct to a frog's leg! And one should pay more serious attention to the green professor's prophecies. I am in love with the world! That is part of understanding its language and recognizing its deeds. The mystery, the mysticism, as humans call the fabric that they themselves, strangers to things, weave over creation, blocking its pores, arises out of the lethargy of their thoughts and feelings. The smallest animal shakes its head about it. The world – listens! Right from the beginning it has been standing wide open for all to see, for the creatures, for every leaf, every pebble, every drop of water from the lakes, rivers, and oceans, and for the tiniest grain of sand on the shore. They can look into it – into the giant sparkling egg. The world is Easter! We are also able to see through the shell of creation, though only those of us with a pure character. "He who is pure in heart will see God." Stars are always falling down to earth, because everything has hatched out, glowing stars, but white ones come from the heights as well and cover the tired world protectively. The

Good Lord asked me once in a dream: "Do you like my world? Then I want to give it to you as a gift!" Since then, it belongs to me, and since then I have had no end of things to do. Namely – looking at it all the time. After all, creation fell right into my lap. By way of contrast, how the creature does exhaust itself breathing it in, emptying the world, which is frothing over. I, however, am beginning to learn much from the tall trees, the leafy patriarchs, especially those with large broad leaves. There is no point in my resisting: the severe frost comes to get me, but so does the tyrannical storm, just like the lovely bird in July, all take me into the auditorium of the world. Every patch of sunlight prances silently and lightly over my hands, and the late summer joins me in searching for kernels on the beechnut bushes. I do like to eat them! Really, I could no longer bring myself to pick a spring branch, yet recently a young tree poured its splendor over me, turning my dark gown into a white dress as if by magic. In comparison with humans, trees are more at one with the soil and have more powerful pith, they are also kinder and more reasonable. What care is shown by plants every year for the other living beings of the world. It shows in their basic color. The smallest bush, the daintiest leaf – we are just accustomed to overlooking it. Both the fresh, light green nuance of spring as well as the subdued shading of July and August refresh our eye. But all creatures have their sense of smell expanded as well by the diversity of autumn, by the spikenard of the loosening light and dark tree bark – and everything begins to breathe with silent prayer or worship. That's it! The bird is frightened by your word, a foreign sound in the Testament of its chirping. Be quiet in the forest, only love is allowed – we kiss each other. . . . The body, in which the soul resides, would disintegrate prematurely without the mortar of autumn or without the warming play of the sun. In earlier times, the soul played with the body just as the sun still plays with the earth: ball. Everything is the image of God – and one should therefore be careful about defiling anything in the world – some of God's soul would like to stream in everywhere, but can only be mirrored in clear places. Perhaps I am being indiscreet by giving away the secret of man and his world. The body is but illusion. And even the body of the world was a fabrication of the first human soul. The body of the world is tough and resilient. But if you should ever feel an earthquake, a passing doubt of the soul about its world illusion, think of me, even if the body of the earth swallows you, in order to spit you out again moments later. The childlike vagaries of the soul when it was still young were to be embodied and remove the core! The babbling rhyme became a deadly serious matter. But that is how the miracle of the fakirs is explained, indeed of all the saints, of the Baal Shem Tov and the other wonderful Rabbis, who were able, through abstinence, to transcend their conquered bodies. The cabala says: "God suffused the world with a mantle of divine light." The cabala is the spiritual landscape, the divine plan of paradise. Wherein we still live today, darkly surrounded by physical delusion in the form of an assumed Garden of Eden. That is the ancient tragedy of the human soul, that its fabricated colossus endangers it. Death itself often hesitates a long while before heaving it off. Take good care of your palace made of the growing illusion of pulsing flesh! But even the poet is able, while still alive, to sweep the stubborn stanza from his soul. This state is called inspiration, making room for God! Above all, however, fervent prayer, praying makes one strong, lifts the longing soul out of its nocturnal illusion and wraps it in a winged dress suitable for the sabbath. Prayer should free you. Be cheerful in your belief! King David danced at the head of the procession before the Ark of the Covenant. – Just as my body stands in my light, so the fabricated body of the world stands in the way of the soul of the world. A third Testament could be written about that. Perhaps then some creature would cry again about the lost paradise. Is there still a small spot of paradise that was not subject to the fabrication of illusion? Perhaps an Eden is waiting for you behind the hedge of the inspiration of this clairvoyant hour. Already freed from step-feelings in the dream of love, the horizons around your soul break away with sweet pain; but to regard the body as arbitrary fiction would be to compose it so negligently as to dismiss it. The assumption of a body proves the presence of the soul, since not even a grain of wheat can take shape without the spirit being present. What separates itself from the soul of God becomes a creature and wants to live somewhere. So the separated soul seeks a home in the shell of its illusion. – Again the ocean is marching over me. I hurry into my house, light the candle on my table, because the evening twilight makes me shiver. I believed I would die before my child and bequeathed him this verse as a relic:

> A solemn star is shining . . .
> That an angel lit for me.
> I never saw our holy city in the Lord,
> It called me often in the dream of the wind.
>
> I have died, my eyes gleam far away,
> My body decomposes and my soul flows
> Into the tear of my now-orphaned child,
> Sown anew in his gentle heart.

I dream – waves come through the walls of my room, through the crack of the door. I hurry to the stretch of water. A seabird couple takes me between them – because – I don't have parents anymore. We glide over the bubbling champagne into the wide, wide world. March has come. The large snowman stands gravely offended before the door of spring. Sometimes he snows, still mixed with the hoarfrost of crocodile tears, in order to annoy the world, but the spring does not let itself be intimidated by him. On the berry tree before my window the corals have shriveled up. Only one is still waiting as a wedding present for a white jackdaw. The corals of the trees, the needles of the spruce, and the few remaining silvery-brown leaves of the popular were my eyes' game and pleasure in the winter. The sparrows woke me early in the morning, coming down from heaven just for that purpose. I am in love with the world. Also with its illusion, which has its own legitimacy. Ask God himself! I long only to incarnate my thoughts and feelings, to express them in words. Therefore, do not destroy my illusion, "or I'll go out of my mind," and I *would* like to experience the summer in its entire extravagant shape from body to body.

THE WALL

A wall rises diagonally in front of my window. Like the stone tablet broken from the peak of the heavenly cliff, my slab grew out of the holy ancestral layer of earth. And it never occurred to me to find out whose house it was the back of, as high and wide as it is. It invites me, overwhelmed, to impress my verses in its crumbling stone, and it reminds me of my school days, because it too was once a child like I was, a small slab, indeed my slate. I put it in my plush green schoolbag; its cute little sponge, dangling back and forth on a string, gazed back at the people through the narrow streets that led to the school. How large my slate has grown! Just now a thick cloud with foamy November water washed it shiny and pure for me. Not for me to learn the ABCs on it or to scratch the numerals of the examples again in squares. – Even the teacher screamed when the slate-pencil slipped out of my hand. I can't

go into that here – the massive slate wall that stands diagonally in front of my arched window longs for MY LITERARY
WORKS, for the fine selection of my blood, for my psalms.
"See, from now on I will be the vineyard of your soul . . ." it
sings joyfully all the way into my heart. And in the future I
want to plant my wine-colored word in the sunshine on the
large stone back, so that it will be eternal! Even if the wall does
block my view of the streets and meadows, it calls my attention to the eternity out of which our Father created the world.
Out of the same kernel the poet forms his figures and breathes
his own life into them. Since living in my room, I have lost all
worldly ambition. In reality, what a petty, short existence my
books and all books lead before moldering away in libraries.
This large body of stone belonging to St. Christopher will
carry my psalm over the entire world into heaven. So that
God will read it. . . . And even if someday all the houses on the
street have fallen into ruin, the immortal slate will remain, the
high wall unshakable in the stone in which I crowned the language, gathered the word, and let its thunder sound. Poets
smile who walk past the wall and do not know what filled
them with joy; to the persecuted it will be a protective back-
ing, because its inextinguishable, invisible inscription is made
from divine material.

THE EAGLE OWL

I have never seen the front face of the wrinkled wall that
stands diagonally before my window. But I have become close
friends with the back. In fact, I have it to thank for a singular
occurrence. Since some of its bricks crumbled entirely away
and fell onto the garden courtyard, a sort of dimple was
formed in the body of the old building, which a homeless bird

soon put to use and with his wife built a nest on the protected building site he had found. I saw daily how the great tit couple collected stems and cobwebs and pulled hair out of half a comb that they found to upholster the inside of their nest. They went through the openings in the wire into the chicken coop in the yard next door, picked up the cozy little feathers that the hens had plucked out of each other, and flew away. I so like to look at the garden courtyard; when one looks carefully, something is always happening, fresh from nature, something that one cannot experience on the street. By August, the two married birds didn't come anymore to fetch bread from my windowsill. The meal that was set out for them remained untouched. And yet, when I peered intently around the corner into the niche in the wall, I saw wings move. I always drink my tea close to the window and particularly love the great tit, whose great-grandparents I admired as a child for their colorful, shimmering plumage. Their favorite food was any kind of cabbage. And those birds were just as dear as these grandchildren, to whom my cuisine no longer seemed to taste good. What else could I assume. In the last few nights I heard an eagle owl screech several times and then again early in the morning, until I was convinced that the eerie bird was really present.

It happened when I was having a snack. A murderer's square head peered out of my little friends' accommodation with two round, evil, unmoving eyes, peered right through my window into my room. I had already taken my handkerchief out of my pocket to cry, when I saw the great tits in the crown of the white poplar, stuffing the little tits' beaks with tasty earthworms. But the eagle owl, too, was watching the parents feed their children; it stepped in front of its house, preened itself, and tried its wings, since it had noticed the remains of my slice of bread and ham on the window ledge. In

33

no time it flew over, its beating wings making a rasping sound. It was no longer the youngest of eagle owls, it suffered from gout. Nonetheless, it devoured the delicacy without so much as a glance in my direction, and withdrew into its stony cave; it had thrown out the coddled down feathers. When the mountain ash tree in the garden courtyard below was full of berries, I often leaned out my window and smiled with it and wished that I could wear such radiant jewelry around my neck. The great tits continued to refrain from letting me feed them. They dug for white meat, fresh from the soil. That's what their brood needed to grow into birds. And only my eagle owl did not abandon me. It had confidence in my cuisine. I would never have asked it to become vegetarian. Today I slept an hour longer than usual, and assume that the eagle owl had sat in front of my windowpane and waited for an hour. And even if I would never have believed in thought transference from person to person, I now believe in a blood telegraphy between humans and animals. Please, I swear to it! To all of you to whom I am telling this event, thereby enriching your knowledge of natural history. In the short, bent beak of the eagle owl swung a small branch of the mountain ash tree with seven dark red berries, held in an umbel. I opened the window as quickly as possible. The predatory bird flew cautiously into my room, placed the magnificent present chivalrously on my plate, as a husband's present to his wife on the morning after their wedding night, and without much to-do he consumed the sardines remaining in the can, eating head and tail, and slurping the aromatic oil into his old, rusty innards. He cleaned his beak, felt satiated, and with an eagle owl screech he sprang away, bursting with blissful joy as in younger years, a happy August bird. Paying scant attention to his ridiculous, narrow, rented apartment in the basement of his world, he sprang away over the roofs of the houses, coming to a dignified rest on his church tower, the peak of which I can see perfectly from my window.

TO THE RUSSIAN CABARET ACT
"THE BLUE BIRD"

Dearest Mr. Jushny, Master of Ceremonies!

This goes beyond dreams! The species to which your blue bird belongs was never seen here before. I'm telling everyone about your blue bird; nothing would please me more than to come every evening to the colorful church service; it fills me with joy. I have already told you, as Master of Ceremonies, that your Cabaret is the first Cabaret Theater that does not have a dirty joke as the treble clef. You are the magician who turns paper into silk, and a painting into flesh and blood. The young lady who plays the violin so outstandingly accompanies all the magic with wonderful music. And you, Grand Duke Jushny, are the gentlest attendant of the blue bird. I was always happy when you stepped forward out of all the shimmer with a delightful surprise in your eye, with a mood full of drumbeats between your hands, and taught us spectators how to applaud. You involved us with the orchestra. I thank you for every minute in your cabaret, the incomparable Blue Bird.

Else Lasker-Schüler

THE THEATER

Dedicated to the Wonderful Professor Max Reinhardt
with the Love of an American Indian

In the first place, let the theater not forget its youth! Once upon a time it too was very small, and played with its first prop. I can empathize with that, in a way I am a theater, too, that has always stayed at the same level. Where a beam lay in the meadow, I climbed on it, or I sprang with joy onto the board that the carpenter had forgotten, a small elevation of the floor in front of our living-room windows. From this seat, one could look through a spyhole and better watch what was happening on the street. This step, as we liked to call the tiny stage, was my favorite piece of furniture in the house. As evening approached, I would get my dear mother to watch, and she became a full audience, who listened with rapt attention to my Karl von Moor, with a feather in my hat and a handkerchief swung over my shoulder.

She was very proud of me. My dear mother's aversion to the theater abated. I grew up, and so did my hobby of playacting. When I surprised my mother by appearing as a living stage – hidden behind a curtain – then she knew; today is the première, in which I played all the parts in the drama I had written myself. My mother was delighted, bolted the door, and enthusiastically praised my voice! I inherited my love of the theater from my father, he usually sat in the first row of the parterre and joined in. That is, he recited the parts, to the amusement of the actors and actresses, who felt particularly at home in our house after the performance. My father spoke like an entire chorus; the sound of his baritone voice reached from one end of the city to the other. For that reason he was always given the so-called shouting roles in the little reading circle that my mother had founded. He forgot his houses and his towers; a horse could not bring him to his office when he had to read "the Franz." With the book *The Robbers* in his hands (often he held it upside down), he hurried through his rooms screaming blue murder. His regiment of shiny polished boots flew into the corners, and the house shook in its strong roots. His voice made music directly; that's why it also flutters on the tip of my tongue. I was just too shy, when my drama *The Wupper* was accepted by the German Theater, to ask that they "hev da Amadeus play wid da glass heart. Dat's why da spice wad missin, da magic in da bouillon." When Paul Lindau congratulated me after the première and perceived that I, the daughter of his roguish old friend Schüler and the youngest child of his adored friend Jeanette Schüler, stood before him in person, he actually cried (and not just theatrical tears) How he had to remind my father, often forcibly, every time he used to threaten in one of his "shouting roles" to smash up the table and chairs, "that he wasn't on a stage; but in a charming living room." I love the theater. If only I had been given a small proscenium box, at least – as an apartment. I would have known how to furnish it. "When I see a stage!! There should always be genuine theater played on it!" In the pubs of the theaters, where my actor friends love to meet after the performance, there was often more real theater played than previously on stage. Where does one still hear the stamping of horses' hooves, thunder and lightning, hail and rebellion? These games are refreshing; and I love the scenery! Bare walls are a waste. The aesthetic leathery stages produce: yawns. Theater is theater! The theater is not a lecture hall for medicine, or for any other faculty. And theater has to do with symbolism – it has a dilettantish effect when the symbolism is put on as a motif, as content of the play. But a good play should *become* a symbol for the audience. Granted, Strindberg, for whom the original letters of the alphabet were symbolism, could permit himself, as he convinced us so often, to make symbolism the content of his literary works. Space and perspective and curving, the brush stroke of feeling – these make the breath of the drama, only they can bring it to life. If one thinks of the flea-pit of a provincial theater, even there it often happens that mixed in with the grandiose drama by

Schiller one finds – eternity. We don't want to wander home-wards after the performance depressed or purified, but shaken by the happiness of the – grief or even the joy. Theater should remain theater.

THE REVOLVING WORLD FACTORY

Whoever has found within himself a tree or a path hardly considers the city in which he lives. And this is particularly true of the creative person who is able, from the lighthouse of his racing heart, to look over a capital city, over Berlin, the endless field of houses.

After all, it is a weakness to place oneself on a green sofa and unpack one's idyll in any surroundings. "To be able to work in peace and quiet." The aestheticists like to flee to – comfortable desolation to write an ode; the photographers among the art-ists, the chatterers with the kid-glove skin. Some friend owns a little house in the country, and it is there that they come to terms with the saucy springtime of their literature. – From far off, wandering bats pass by their gardens in Greek robes. San-dal strings flutter in front of their legs, and rich poetry pours from their lips. They carry it in nets, the fruit of knowledge. – Damn it all, it really is courageous to make one's way through the diversity of the crowd into the center of the city. We artists are, after all, creative people, the material lies within us. Does God, for instance, retreat to a village? Like the aesthetically creative person – who discloses his novel of a soul on the pasture in Worpswede or the Lüneburg Heath. Or like Ama-deus Müller, who parades his natural hair through the open spaces of the suburbs in May. . . .

This Berlin, revolving world factory. Tempo: the inhabit-ants run on reels; it is either nerve-racking for them, or they understand how to organize themselves out of it and become mechanical. At any rate, they are more likeable than the small-town dwellers (present company excepted), who creep around on their bellies. – There is a more glowing welcome here for the person who has remained human, who can unfasten the wheels from his shoes again; that is the test to which he is subjected by the big city. If he passes the test, he remains alive – that testifies to his worth. As with money. The rich man need by no means become a devil, let alone a sentimental safety-deposit box, a tipsy barbarian. Attention!! In the person, however, who is incapable of exuding his "mental" wealth, on *that* cold "Satan" the eternal soul freezes to death. My love for the city of Berlin, for all large cities, of course does not in any way exclude my love for the meadows and forests. I am enraptured more than anyone by everything that grows on earth, and collect the acorns and chestnuts and berries, all the flowering toys on the paths, and protect the blade of grass from the brutality of the step. The water is my playmate, with its shells and its seaweed. But for writing and drawing what I need most of all and of all things is *me*. I wait in vain for myself, for my morning. What love will shine over my heart and evoke in me the blossom of the word: poetry.

For a long time I have picked nothing more from the vineyards of my life, and yet I breathe the same breath. Has the difficult time asphalted my heart, or did real breath blow out its sun? I am groping in the dark.

Neither the big city, nor any city at all, nor any village anywhere on earth has anything to do with a production; but people do, often a single person. From our large city sounds the scream, the roar of technology; the fear of death wears a warning face behind made-up, empty masks, but the longing climbs up right away into the moon. Our city Berlin is strong and terrible, and its wings know where it wants to go. That is why the artist returns – again and again, to Berlin, *here is the clock of art*, which is neither slow nor fast. This reality is already mystical.

One cannot overcome the friend's apostasy. It is an operation that leaves one in danger of bleeding to death. Even my house and his house were connected with nerves. My heart celebrates the burial. Friendship in the big city: the artist's consolation, *Love*, however, is his revelation, *ascension*. Only *this* voyage is necessary for the artist to be able to create.

LILY REIFF

Here one can maintain in the true sense of the music: *C'est le ton qui fait la musique.* Lily's fingers lure mellow tones from the ivory of the keys. The one grand piano looks jealously over at the preferred one, on which Lily Reiff usually plays in the evening hour. Powerful, sweet, and full of fragrance, yes, her tone-poems do have a scent; some smell piously of incense. Best of all I liked to sit, when I was at her hospitable home in Zürich, somewhere hidden behind a portière and listen to her wonderful playing until I found myself in a long since paled past, which now lit up again – lost in reverie between magic brooks and miraculous flowers. I am no music critic; I understand nothing of key signatures and treble clef; I hear the music actually without ears, like a plant. And to criticize seems schoolmasterly to me, because music penetrates my pores, possessing not only my soul but also my body. Lily's music lifts my spirits, it is a swarm of colorful notes in all kinds of sweet diversities. But Lily Reiff is also able to play up a storm, to conjure up a thunderstorm; then there is suddenly thunder and lightning under her beautiful hands. I have been asked, as is usual, whether her compositions that she played for me were modern or old-fashioned. What does that mean, modern or old-fashioned music? Music still in the rough, or music polished, that is how I understand the difference in music, as in all the arts. *Genuine music is immortal!* The compositions by the wonderful musician – she is no virtuoso – are full of reverence and a repeatedly resplendent springtime; a few music flowers, hospitably extended notes, are what one takes home for life. In Germany recently one of her two operas was produced with great success.

DOCTOR DOLITTLE AND HIS ANIMALS

*(Translated from the English by
Edith L. Jacobsohn-Schiffer)*

When I met Edith L. Jacobsohn-Schiffer head over heels I called her Gladys. With her monocle wedged in bewilderment in her lightning-blue eye, she studied me, as I did her, like newborn children. It happened this way: some impatient person suddenly ripped open the telephone door of the old "Café of the West" and I flew head over heels out of the telephone booth onto the other stool of the little marble table, at which a female gentleman was sitting, that is – the gold-blond Gladys. It happened so quickly we had no time at all to think. That is how people should always meet, with introductions left to chance, from right out of the blue, or head over heels from the telephone booth. I am so accustomed to calling Edith Jacobsohn *Gladys,* I naturally mean by *Gladys* Edith Jacobsohn, the translating lady, translator of the delightful, thrilling book by the English author and illustrator Hugh Lofting. "I dedicate this book to all children, children in years and children at heart." For the first time, I looked forward for three evenings to going to bed. Propped on my pillow, I read until two in the morning, the windowpanes frosted over, a small moon above my bed, engrossed in the plot, the powerful, sweet book: *Doctor Dolittle and His Animals.* To give away the plot would be to rob the reader of the events of the stories and of the comical drawings. For three years in a London girls' grammar school, Gladys, the eternal schoolgirl, learned all the ins and outs of the English language and was able to translate for us this interesting, loving book in sound and color from the English. The Englishman says: "It is very truly translated, indeed."

THE LAMAS

When bells ring softly through the corridors of the hotel "The Saxon Inn," the lamas are praying together in front of their magnificent, consecrated Buddha carpet. Of late, they have been seriously including me in their prayers. They inhabit almost the entire third floor of the fine, most homelike hotel: The Saxon Inn, in which I have lived for many years now. It received me hospitably, too, and I grew fond of it, like an international home. Between Tibetan priests next door I listen devoutly to deep, foreign ceremonies. Songs that are dear to the lamas, that they droning roll out again and again with the holy prayer mat, to bring the mountains magically closer, to enter the homeland from whose heights they descended, leaving its monasteries in order to see another part of the earth. Until then, reaching here would have seemed to them a dream voyage to the evening star, inexplicably come true. At the moment, Europe is taking place for our religious Asian guests in our hotel "The Saxon Inn," a fertile planet that accommodates them lavishly and considerately. The Tibetans have the starry fairy Anny to thank, a blue-eyed young lady staying on the same floor, for the large number of German words that their fine lips now can shape, and receive, as a pleasant result, tea, cake, and cigarettes. The dalai lama usually takes his tea from his own gold-trimmed cup. Delightful, when he knocks at my door in his red ceremonial robe and courteously explains in response to my startled come in!: "The Supreme Lama!! Good Morning." Stretched out, or resting on his silk cushion with crossed thighs and folded feet, he follows, enraptured, the bell-like sounds of the rhythms of Buddha and strolls in spirit already over the resounding paths that the young monks prepare for him with their voices, he strolls alive into nirvana. The door of the widest hotel room, where the little Tibetan community gathers for prayer, stands slightly open most of the time. I think their dalai master loves it when others secretly participate. They are dear, childlike people, devout and wise, who came to us from the heights of their country; quiet flowers entwine themselves around their sunny hearts, and their gentle velvet eyes are like the holy eyes of the cows that are their primal deities. Sometimes a roguish side surfaces in the trusting young monks, then they run with outstretched arms through the corridors of the hotel, frightening everyone with their ceremonial devils' masks that they wear in Tibet for monastery festivals; until their *bogdahan,* the highest priest, smilingly admonishes them to be quiet. Their glowing hearts suppress their mischievous mood, but it still shines in the singing of their choir. We in the hotel want to make them happy, to surprise them with presents. Hardly any European is capable of fathoming the depth of their being; I would give a great deal to be able to speak their language, at least to read the words that reveal themselves in the peace of Buddha as faint blood-colored scars at the entrance to their heart. One must understand how to read between the eyelashes of their soul. Certainly the dalai lama, who has achieved enlightenment, is able to bring about events that I have often seen described in books written by people who have traveled through Tibet.

The lamas really enjoy riding in the company car through the streets of Berlin. One after another they climb into the big car in their tall fur hats, each of them a little Mount Everest. And last of all the dalai lama, with his exceptional dignity, calmly enters the waiting car, where the best seat is reserved for him. They had already visited England and France before they became our guests. Next to the hotel "The Saxon Inn," in the theater in Nollendorf Square, one can attend the lamas' religious celebrations and dances. Their trumpets are about ten meters long, and their solemnity floats over the entire earth.

IN THE SMALL ROSEWOOD BOX

*In Commemoration of the Hundredth Anniversary
of Goethe's Death*

My mother, whom I admired, possessed in addition to her Napoleon collection a passionate reverence for Goethe. He and she, from one and the same city, born in Frankfurt, encountered each other under the sky of memory, on the paths of their attractive hometown. Although the poet had long since been continuing to write his divine verses in Olympus, the eternally admired one nevertheless lived on earth in the glowing heart of my mother. Without my mother, I would not have been able to imagine what Goethe was like. Whether my rapturous young mother was in love with him or with Bonaparte the great emperor, I am still unable to determine. But I certainly knew even as a child that Goethe was the poet of her pure heart. That was testified to by the many poems written down in flourishing handwriting in the large autograph album. My mother's handwriting was tropical, the letters began to bloom. The lines of Goethe's poetry became resplendent avenues. Just now I was leafing through the treasured book and remembered a letter that the young Goethe once wrote to Friedericke. The precious commemorative page, never published, lay preserved in a small carved rosewood box in the wall cupboard under lock and key. For me as a child, it increased in value, in the belief that Goethe had written it to her. That moved me to honor the copy that was made for each of my sisters.

Tenderly loved Friedericke.

Winter threatens to envelop us with starry flakes and your Goethe thinks more longingly of the unforgettable sweet hours with her, the divine one, (several words illegibly faded) bedded in her childlike lap, when unfortunately, uninvited guests positioned themselves around us lovers on the meadow. Soon you, my magnanimous girlfriend, will receive a copy of my "Dorothea." In her you should discover similarities with your disposition. Meanwhile, I expect from my much loved Friedericke sincere praise after the suspense of reading. Your Goethe is carrying your valuable present with great delight in his neckerchief. The delightful garnet winks seductively at the ladies. Don't become jealous, my dear (several words illegibly faded) Goethe, your (several words illegibly faded) a loyal lover and by no means a horrible womanizer, as bad friends so like to call him.

> He who plays with life
> Never gets ahead.
> He who does not command himself
> Always remains a slave.
>
> Your faithful Goethe.

In those days, some people doubted the validity of this letter to Friedericke; others wanted to maintain that the four-lined poem at the end stemmed from his later period; but in any case it was Paul Lindau who dedicated the precious document to my marvelous mama. – Once a week the little reading circle met at our house in the evening. My papa got the roles with shouting in them! My mother read the part of Gretchen in *Faust*, if one of the two female singers, Lucca or Elmenreich, didn't happen to be contributing to the hospitable mood of our house. The literati of Elberfeld gathered around the big round table. My two charming sisters, fifteen-year-old Martha Theresia and fourteen-year-old Annamarie, sat beside each other in a niche behind a stained-glass window and listened with rapt attention. I was allowed to sleep on the sofa in the little adjoining room; I was so afraid of being all alone in the uppermost story of our wide, eerie house. Men came from the forest, butchers, they came down the steep slope and sang so harshly, in many voices. The reading circle paused, offended, just when they were reading about . . . love. Only my papa's voice, swelling to a chorale, could not be drowned out, his thundering organ, a true hurricane. He was reciting Mephistopheles in exactly the same ecstasy that he used for Schiller's "Franz the Villain." The door to my provisional bedroom was slightly ajar, and through the crack I heard the reading circle burst into laughter. Even my well-behaved sisters could not control themselves, especially when my parents' daily guest, Paul Lindau, passed a drink to my papa with the most hilarious irony, bringing my father back down to earth with Faustian words: "Now I have also studied philosophy through and through with concerted effort." – But when it was time for my mother's role, they were quiet as mice. She thought I was long since asleep. I was eight years old and often still sat in her lap between the small locket pictures of her parents cut in coral. And she told me that Grandmama and Grandpapa had seen Johann Wolfgang von Goethe ice-skating.

When I read in the *Berlin Daily News* a few years ago that the famous physician had died, a little story occurred to me about the wonderful doctor and me and a Mexican Indian I had been carrying around with me for two and a half weeks in my – stomach. The Privy Councillor held my letter in his hand as he opened the doors to the waiting room, and it seemed as if he were looking for – the writer, me. "My Dear Privy Councillor Bumm. I am the poet Else Lasker-Schüler and would like to consult you, but I live on air and love, and even this is very scarce. May I come *anyway?* Else Lasker-Schüler" . . . suddenly he took my hand and led me into his consulting room, in front of the big bright window.

"First let me take a look at you, my dear patient, I have never seen a poet before!" And the Privy Councillor looked at my eyes, my lips, my nose, even my ears and their little twisted rings, and then my forehead, "the lighthouse, of course," he said. "And now, dear poet, what is your complaint?" I began first of all to tune the strings like the violinist in the orchestra, I mean, I invented stories; the doctor's attentiveness, however, hastened the harmony of my ballad of what really happened. "Privy Councillor, I am actually quite healthy, because the pressure that I (I pointed to my stomach) have felt for two and a half weeks has a natural cause. I swallowed a medallion in the form of a little heart." "How did that come about, dear poet?" "I was strolling along Linden Avenue by myself, and just as I was turning into the big arcade, I noticed a small heart lying on the sidewalk." "What type of metal was it made of?" asked the professor seriously. "*To me* it seemed to be made of flesh and blood, and I picked it up quickly to protect it from harm. And as I carefully bent back its half-opened heart chambers," I said with pride, "I looked into a face, Privy Councillor, such as I had never seen in my entire life. Even though the colored photograph in the frame was very small, I was nevertheless enchanted to make out the palm-green, long-lashed, deep-set, somber eyes beneath an angular forehead." "And what color was his hair?" the physician interrupted. "Lizard black, Privy Councillor." "And what did you find in the other heart chamber, dear poet?" "In the left heart chamber, Privy Councillor, stood his worthy name: Bengal Tiger of the Pumas. How long I stood in front of one of the stores or in the middle of the road of the arcade, I cannot say. I was possessed by the sight of the Indian chief; when spears of sharp eyes hit me, I woke up and shrank together to a hazelnut that contained only one thought. The policeman had noticed my fine theft, the precious little heart beat in my hand with my big heart. The guard moved. In no time I swallowed my dear find, jealous as I am. But, Privy Councillor, I have realized that it will be impossible to celebrate a union in my stomach. Ow!!" I have had to scream with pain so often in recent days and nights. Compassionately and understandingly the kind professor examined me – at least he won't squash it – and I breathed a sigh of relief when he had arrived at the tips of my lungs. I carry his prescription in a lace handkerchief in my jacket pocket as a talisman, a wonderful-sounding verse:

Corde alieno vulnerata
atque oleao crotonis liberata.

(Wounded by a foreign heart, relieved by croton oil.)

KOLBERG

*(Before one was threatened there by people
wearing swastikas)*

The whole winter long I thought of the ocean. I have been to all beaches and to several in actuality. But always with a belt

48

of algae and starfish around my smock, exactly like Friday wore. I walked along the quiet and the loud ocean, was at the Black Sea and the Red Sea, found corals, even dreamed under tall Jerusalem cherry trees. A diver took me with him to the bottom. I collected mussels and stones, picked living roses and carnations, played the fishes' favorite party game with them in their watery home:

> Liver is from a pike
> And not from the sardine.
> The most beautiful fish was Engelbrecht –
> Who is drying on the sand-dune.

whereupon a charming little goldfish began by whispering to the tragic carp:

> Liver is from a pike,
> Whose life was not robust.
> He rhymed well, he rhymed poorly
> And died of the trochee.

It was entertaining down there, I didn't want to come back to the surface ever again, I had become so salty. People around me still feel thirsty. How am I related to the ocean – through a weakness on the side of my great-grandfather or my great-grandmother – I am unable to check the water level. Certainly I rise when the ocean is mentioned. In the winter, I often stood at the Stettin train station, my face turned toward Pomerania – there the most beautiful beach on the Baltic Sea awaits me anew each year. But it was so cold on the unheated platform that my feet were frozen to the inside of my boots along each side, and I hurried the kilometers back on the ice-cold leather of the soles to my cabin right up in the sea of clouds in the most gentlemanly hotel in Nollendorf Square. I love the Baltic seaside resort, Kolberg in Pommern. I made friends with the ocean there and with its green-eyed friend, the forest. We three are the arch Indians and swore the oath of allegiance. From time immemorial I have carried sap from the bark in my blood and the joy of the blooming playthings of all trees in my heart; above all, though, the eternally old burgundy of the ocean is stored in the cool vessel of my main artery, now calm and then rising up again most ceremoniously. For all injuries, the advice of the Heinrichsdorf medical service is there in Kolberg. – As a child, I believed that Pomerania had burned down long ago, as it says in the song. How a folk song can lead one astray! Words, that like mussels are thrown up on the beach by waves and then collected by a poet in his little pail. That is fundamentally how a folk song originates. Sometimes, lying between the mussels is an amber word with a scarab of a fly embedded in it. Between the tall chimneys of my home-town, my little toy clock played: Ladybird, ladybird, fly away home,* and so on. – There is in all swelling truth a Pomerania, and its capital city on the sea is called Kolberg. It wears the most majestic jewelry of the Baltic Sea, which has its ebb and flow in the great pearl. – Soon I will be roaming around again in my Kolberg, walking barefoot down the dunes, watching the action of the water as it pulls down the tallest sand castles; the most powerful waves come up and hit against the rocks where we Wild West Robinsons go swimming. From the direction of the forest, curious eyes peer at the beach, looking out through secluded boughs covered with glassy berries. But nakedness has long been the practice for swimming outdoors,

*The German children's song to which Lasker-Schüler is referring is

Maikäfer flieg!	Beetle, fly away!
Dein Vater ist im Krieg.	Your father is at war.
Deine Mutter ist in Pommerland.	Your mother is in Pomerania.
Pommerland ist abgebrannt.	Pomerania has burned down.
Maikäfer flieg!	Beetle, fly away!

and everyone swims in this manner, even the ladies whose dress otherwise follows the latest fashion. – Having just arrived, I am already walking up and down the deck in the sea. Over the long bridge with red lights to the ruler-edge horizon, I hurry onto the ship where the visitors to the spa are enjoying a late evening stroll. Music, the calls of invisible birds who glide past, they come from the little temple, from the spa grounds. Each of the players is in the true sense of the tone a musician. When the barcarole from "Tales of Hoffmann" is on the program, my heart lifts into the heavens, comes home blue – but it does come home – at eight o'clock for dinner. They already know – but I nevertheless eat my evening meal afterwards in my guesthouse in the Villa Agnes, my guesthouse that has never yet been there but is always returning. At the beginning of my stay, I take my food and drink alone under the big open umbrella in the front garden of the white house, until I have overcome my fear of possibly sitting across from someone or beside someone. One does meet men often, and women, who run their tongue along their teeth while digesting their food, who make fluting and groaning sounds through their "have a good dinner" cheeks and their front and back and now sour milk teeth. Don't think that I am crazy, but these noises drive me around the bend. And the people on staff here are really concerned that I and all the guests be provided with care and attention in the most magnificent of all villas, where one seeks refuge to quiet one's nerves once and for all. To the owner of the guesthouse, our charming hostess Frau H., a stein containing the entire cellar of the sea, the second to her friend Frau von G., the kind vice-principal. And let us sing again the national anthem of the Villa Agnes:

> In the black whale of Askalon
> Two ladies now direct the pension
> With care and special tact

51

And a great gift for sensitivity.
Thus they engaged Frau Benz to the department
Last year in May
To keep house.
She cooks meals that refresh and delight us.

In front of the hospitable house stands a small pyramid, the ivy-covered monument that the mourning, grateful citizens of Kolberg erected in memory of their beloved doctor and captain Hirschfelden, the father of the Villa Agnes. The Villa Agnes now accommodates many visitors from all countries. A picture of the doctor as a young man greets the children at the round table in the little dining room. But upstairs in my study (last year I worked there toward my Doctor of Ocean, D.Oc.) hangs the last photograph of that great, benevolent man. He has the only type of beard that I like, a captain's beard. It washes powerfully around his kind face and once wafted away all pain. – Month after month more people come to Kolberg. It is an international concern: Russians, Poles, Czechs, Swedes. The little town, soon grown up, is becoming a city. In the ballrooms of the hotel there is dancing and festivity; and an entertaining nightclub right beside our villa. In the cafés, the visitors place their stomachs on ice. The stores in the city and on the beach outdo themselves. In the bookstores the most modern books are on display (my books are also available . . .). But I myself do not read, preferring to look at the agates and flintstones, the aventurine, the amethysts and garnets in the stone store on the way to the beach, but best of all I like to visit the mussel lady. In her store window I admire the pretty little mussel boxes, the mirrors in mussel frames, the clock stands, the transparent little green and red bags with mussels to play with, but also the rough pink ones that people place around their fountains or as protection around the edge of their lawns. In Kolberg, one starts to play again; becomes quite young and sturdy, and drinks one's caraway brandy at Preißler's from the fount of life before going to bed.

"To be fair, there are, in addition to Kolberg, three other Baltic Sea spas on Usedom Island that I can recommend: Herringsdorf, Ahlbeck, and Swinemünde." Thus spake the doctor and captain – so the old Kolberg fisherpeople tell me. The ocean, too, has a wide sand stage just like the Kolberg – the theater here in the forest diagonally across from our nice villa, with performances that are not to be scoffed at. After the theater I love to take a walk alone along the sea, in silence and at peace with the world. If only I weren't discovered so often by a melancholy composer on the Steinway grand or by a writer with the extra olive leaf in his beak! I like to walk there beside the great water and know why I am sad. . . . But in the garden of roses and colorful foxglove the next day at noon there is plenty of sun again from the golden mama and I fly then with great joy in my heart past the Persante, the small stream that runs through the city, over the bridge to Grünhausen, to the carousel. The children on holiday from the almshouses are drinking yogurt in the inn gardens, and I sit down between them. They know I will also let them ride on the carousel. It is improper to no longer be a child. Every evening, secretly (there is a fine of six hundred marks if it's found out), I slip the entire ocean into my little pocket, and put the endless piece of water jewelry in a case under my pillow.

The flag has already been hoisted at the lighthouse, I'm coming!

MY WUPPER

I probably made my heart flow when I wrote my play *The Wupper*. It was in the night, I was sleeping, yes I was sleeping. My brain, therefore, was not able to conduct me, to give the beat to my little globe. A stage play must always be a world, in

53

order to roll. Not, for example, to reach the stage. Whoever thinks of that or can think of that even if only secretly when creating something, makes a world but does not create it. Skillfulness is not magic. Conjuring things up is the poet's craft.

LETTER TO JESSNER

My dear Manager and Artistic Director Leopold Jessner!

Allow me to say a few more words before the performance of my *Wupper:*

My play *The Wupper* is a genuine gift, a small world. It is my belief that if you, the Manager and Artistic Director, were not also convinced of this fact, you would not go to the trouble of making my *Wupper* flow again. Now I, after all, created it, am its creator and see it from the water perspective. Every play is probably a world, an image of the author. Thus, when I regard my play from all sides, from top and bottom, I clearly recognize its similarity to me, even if my drama turned out blond and bright-eyed! Also, at that time I spoke the low Elberfeld accent on the stage of my heart, otherwise I couldn't communicate with the people of the Wupper Valley; they came and went, ha'en't ya seen 'em! Some of them I first had to get to know myself. I became secretly fond of Amadeus, the deepest of the three vagabonds. Indeed, if I had not unfortunately been born as Else Lasker-Schüler – in the fourth courtyard of the seventh heaven – I would be Amadeus, united with his colleagues, in the corner of the night. So who should play *him?* I myself would like to lead you, the Manager and Artistic Director, through the wide streets and narrow alleyways of my play, to reveal to you the secrets of the city, to let you have a taste of the black Wupper River, and you will see that my *Wupper* in short cannot be called a fairy tale or a play or a drama, at most a city ballad with smoking chimneys and signals. The Wupper River of the city of Elberfeld is the artery of the workers. This central pulse should also not be missing from the set – with the main emphasis on life! The poem, the lyric poetry, that which hangs in the air, the moon in the blue or black cloud of the play. Artistic mood, natural bad mood: silence without rustling, noise without method. To direct a play one needs the skills of a military commander. Max Reinhardt made it flow. Up until then he had stood on the opposite bank, imagining me to be a lady from a girls' high school, who had wafted away from the Roswita ballroom. A play is a creature, a creature can be a world, "tum tingelingeling," my *Wupper* is a creature, a creation, a world, that I myself do not entirely like, frankly. Just because of that, however, I cannot deny that my *Wupper* is a world – to put it modestly – for someone who has not yet traveled all too far. I am concerned about my world, it is being put on for the second time in the theater heaven. A director hasta unnerstan' the astrology uv directshun, 'n' in ma opinyun, he also hasta hava drop uv blood in his basin. 'Cause some of the acts at the fair simply are danjrus. Ah unnerstan' about knife-fightin' 'n' the riders who ride the carrasel; the director even hasta get the Fat Lady Rosa under control. The noise and the nagging! Sumpin' is takin' shape on stage, the throngs are already on the fairgrounds: a quite ordered, even though wild symphony. On stage, people "want" to be something, and something that always succeeds in real life can easily slip out of their paws. And now something else: the curtain! The curtain should only fall in the rarest cases; often not even at the end. After all, life is not over before the end of the world, and *then* there is still the chaos. When the curtain falls, one loses touch with the facts of the matter and falls out of the situation, it makes one tired, numbs the spectator. At least I can never properly get back to the stage again. And yet I am not at all so exceptionally stupid.

55

Since the play is a small, round world – namely, when the people roll with laughter – it is inorganic to have it continually going light and dark. On our earth it is only day and night *once*, and don't remind me that an author once let an eclipse occur in his production. The director should confidently let himself be guided by the illumination of the big world. All of our human brains would be even more nervous, and our eyes would be blind, if the world curtain went up and down more than once a day. It brings one – simply put – out of the situation. I likewise disapprove of artsy and craftsy things on stage: between sweet or tinted rags: the *venerable backdrop?* The backdrop is so grown together with the actor and his audience that it cannot simply be torn down. The actor relaxes in the paper forest, in which he breathes in and out for decades. When breathed on by Karl von Moor,* the paper forest *lives* and is no longer just of cardboard. It served Shakespeare's resurrected kings as a place to return from the world of spirits. It is a mésalliance to combine the subject matter with the backdrop. Aesthetics and genius are not a compatible couple. The world is not constructed of stuff, at best – of houses of cards. I would be capable, as the owner of a theater, of having a curtain constructed of heavy cardboard, or of a piece of blotting paper, or of a tissue paper – behind it the play carries on, before it the spectator fantasizes.

My dear Manager and Artistic Director! I am convinced, this time my *Wupper* will be even better! For me at least, Wupper!! It is not *allowed* to be a flop, so that the people will come to us afterwards and say, "if only we had gone to the movies instead." Manager and Artistic Director,

Your most obedient servant
Prince Jussuf of Thebes

*Karl von Moor is the main character in Schiller's play *The Robbers*.

P.S. For Posterity!
In 1910, the highly respected director *Heinz Herald* discovered my world: *The Wupper*, and I have his energetic will and his help with the staging to thank most sincerely for its appearance in theater heaven.

A LETTER TO WILLEM SCHMIDTBONN

Dear Willem!

Ah've heard da' Dr. Rockenbach wants ta publish a special issue ba' you, 'n' Ah congratulate ya on da', dear Willem, 'n' wish ya great joy 'n' health 'n' a long, entertainin' life; do ya hear me! From doggerel, neither of us has earned a Prussian silver piece, your full honor 'n' recognition, 'n' dat's also worth sumpin', sumpin' spiritual, even if one can't eat it. Waddaya sayda dat, Willem? Ah've been lookin' fer ya now fer most half a dozen years a'ready, 'n' find ya not in da world. Where are ya den actually, Willem, so dat Ah don't get ta feelin' uncanny aroun' ma heart. Three times, namely, ma cuckoo clock has run down 'n' always on da fift hour'a dark midnight. Where are ya actually, Willem? Praps in Hunsrück 'n' wearin' a muzzle? Or are ya sweepin' away da snow wid a broom in da Vosges Mountains? Or are ya stayin' wid da Lorelei 'n' breakin' yo' flamin' heart in two? Ah in any case do not know what it's suppose ta mean 'n' wha Ah'm so sad,* yer always wobblin' in a rockin' chair throo ma thoughts. Da evenin's cool 'n' ma hands'r splashin' unda ma chin, Ah am in Zürich and suddenly – there is a thin coating of ice over ma face. . . . Those were da days, those were da days!

Your Friend

*This is an echo of Heinrich Heine's famous poem, "The Lorelei," which begins with the lines: "Ich weiß nicht, was soll es bedeuten, / Daß ich so traurig bin" (I don't know what it means, I am so sad).

HOW I CAME TO DRAW

Probably this way: my letters of the alphabet burst into bloom – overnight; or to put it better: over the night of the hand. One simply doesn't know – in the darkness of the miracle.

When I look over a grassy place as over a round arc full of green letters or over an autumn garden, full of the rustling writing of the hand of the earth, of the certificate of God, then the riddle is solved. – How I came to draw? Exactly as foliage longs for the flower, so the longing of my living letters conjures up the picture in all colors. It cannot be forced. . . . Many a person, however, may wait confidently for the May of his handwriting.

AN OPEN LETTER TO THE MINISTER OF FINANCE, DR. REINHOLDT

My Dear Retired Minister.

I still remember exactly what you once wrote in the *Leipzig Daily News* about my literary works and – how I recite them. With reference to that, I am requesting an audience with you very soon, Mr. Minister. That is how my letter of last year began, I think it was also in April, the sun wasn't shining, but I shone, and seemed to be on the right track. That you have just been made Minister of Finance comes just at the right time for me, Mr. Minister. It is tremendous of the state to oblige me in this manner! You were still wearing the same watch-chain around your neck as you did in Leipzig, and you have kept the kind, intelligent facial expression that you had then, Mr. Minister. I was observing you from my leather armchair to yours, without your noticing. We spoke like old acquaintances; creative writers have always met each other sometime up in the moon. You suspected that I came on account of my colorful but quite crumbling city of Thebes, to venture a possible loan. You winked so nicely with your eyes, and I rode in thought on my old camel Amm, the flag of victory in my hand, back to my run-down palace. You promised me, Mr. Minister, to do what it is possible to do. I have written fifteen books and one manuscript, and three paperback works (not yet written down) are gathering dust in my head. Isn't that a pity? "A terrible pity!" you stressed, Mr. Minister Reinholdt. If I am not mistaken, both of us even wept about it. Then you began to ask me: whether I was not exhausted by all my "sorting out of things"? My pamphlet that I sent you the day before yesterday: "I'm sorting things out," aimed at my publishers, was in your hands. You held it up and observed me, the bagpipe-player, on the cover. The pamphlet, Mr. Minister, is the cause of Thebes' falling into ruin. I have dedicated myself for years exclusively to the mission that is sacred to me, and have dedicated myself again and again enthusiastically to broadcasting my accusation, which contains the complaints of all writers, dead and alive. Just look at me, how unfashionably I am dressed and what a turmoil I am in and ! ! you should see my closet, everything topsy-turvy, as I throw it in quickly. If I want to send away one of the pamphlets, all kinds of things come tumbling out of the compartment with it: handkerchiefs, stockings, ribbons, my Thebaic play crown, my delightful little porcelain ornaments, the little birdcage, my watering can, my snake in the egg, Jupiter Däubler's Râh, and last of all my massage roller. I can bet my life on it that one of my velvet books will fly out and hit me on the head every time I open my closet. Associations were founded! The writers' association got new wallpaper, the kitchen was equipped, the bathroom manicured. A crooked lawyer established himself in the center, "I am sorting things out," for writers who,

armed with my trusting text, ride up to him in the elevator!!
All behind my back! In the end the German *Writer's Group of
Allotment Gardens* – grows my red Sorting Out–Dreaming
Out in a flowerpot as the only poetry in their flowerbed.

"Welcome, Buddenbrooks and son!
Mr. Fulda held the toast to the ladies as a gentleman,
Ricarda? was there!
She smiled in embarrassment.
A boy came to sweep away all the iambs!
Susannâh, Vizepostata,
The Saulus Werfel Rabunâ
'To you my heart' . . . everything in cash."
Hauptmann replaces Benzmann,
Holz became Scholz.
And God Leonhard stresses:
"The person with side-whiskers is good."*

With the request that you finally deal with the Thebaic question, I sign, to the sound of drums and bells,

Your obedient Prince of Thebes,
Jussuf

THINGS ASKED AND ANSWERED

Answers

Highly Respected Poet!
Writers who get together, who gather together to sit in
judgment, are sacred. They form an *angels' court*. . . . A few

*Lasker-Schüler names, mimics, or alludes to key figures in the Prussian
Writers' Academy, among others Thomas Mann (Buddenbrooks), Ricarda Huch, Franz Werfel, Gerhardt Hauptmann, Arno Holz, and Scholz,
who was president of the academy from 1926 to 1928.

years ago I was aglow with the pamphlet that I wrote against my publishers: "I'm sorting things out" – it was like a mission for me. When I have a mission, I have no fear of the consequences, no matter how heatedly they have been portrayed to me by friends. The whole press took note of my legitimate and honest complaint, quite to my benefit and the benefit of writers in a similar situation. Not long after the appearance of my little book, organizations were formed for the purpose of fighting against the unfair publishers: even the Pen-Club, staged by the assiduous Feist-Wollheim, chatted carefully and aesthetically over tea about incidents with publishers. Persuaded by one of the members of the Pen-Club, I was present, dressed up as Mack the Knife of the Threepenny Opera, at one of their tenderly poetic twilight-hour get-togethers. One evening, the writers' and academics' Christmas star did rise over Germany, in the good winds blown by my pamphlet; but they forgot to invite the author of said pamphlet to the celebration. Did I not write well enough for them. . . ? Is that a reason – in the face of these eminent authorities? When they sit assembled in flashes of inspiration, the high – crocheted lace! – of poetry – "Answer!!"

Yet, it is actually valid to complain about publishing matters. But I complained about all of them with razor-sharpness in my pamphlet: "I'm sorting things out." Organizations, associations, clubs, and in the end the Academy of Poetry grew out of the ground, and right now the most unconcerned, thoughtless publishers continue to stroll undisturbed under the palm trees of our poetry. Very loving greetings, dear poets, from your

Else Lasker-Schüler

SURVEY

What is your opinion on § 218 of the Criminal Code?

Paragraph 218, probably the one forbidding abortion?? I suspect?

What doesn't breathe yet, is not alive; the adverse affects for the "person carrying the child" – are her private affair! But why are harmless means not sold publicly? Besides, only female judges should have a say about this paragraph, since as is well known *men have never yet in their lives gotten as far as the ninth month.*

Else Lasker-Schüler

THE BUTTERFLY

A true story

Klaus said it was dead. But I lifted the little lost butterfly up off the sand-dune and placed it between my hands, a warm little house. Now and then I breathed some July wind through the cracks between my fingers, but the poor butterfly wings remained withered, they that once, the color of a lemon, competed with the rays of the sun. And my friend Klaus asked me if I perhaps intended to bring the dead little animal back to life. Without saying a word, I took it home with me into the garden, where my companion and I usually had our meals, close to the Baltic Sea; one heard the sound of the water even in its tiniest mussel. "If only it would stop the sound of its waves for a while" and my butterfly could wake up in peace on the rose leaf that I smoothed out for it before I put it down on it beside my plate at the set table. Now and then I breathed over its perished little body to awaken it. Besides, it was the sun's birthday today and it awaited the butterflies in their golden dresses and silver shoes. It was glittering festively everywhere. As for her smallest admirer, did she have any idea that he, making his way briskly toward her with joyous enthusiasm, had an accident and was crushed by the sole of a foot? "Certainly, I want to play God," I said seriously in response to my dining companion's mocking question, "what other means do I have of bringing my dead butterfly back to life?" I actually did feel God streaming from all my pores, which put breath into the little dead creature. This is the way one person should strive to replace God on earth for another person, that is, to push oneself to the limit, to perfect oneself, to do God credit, to illuminate his image brightly and not distort it – in one's own soul. And we are responsible for his animals and the blossoming and wilting of his flowers, which one should not throw out in the garbage between rags and broken glass, but should give back to the soil behind the fence. Even the stones should be praised, which keep our step upright and carry us from place to place. I breathed again very carefully, and Klaus, although smilingly at first, put his breath at my disposal, then he breathed gently over the butterfly, after he wove a protective hedge of slender fingers of larkspur around our sacred butterfly. And on our knees, we both awaited the awakening of the smallest Lazarus in front of the rosy vault of the bending petal. Klaus confessed to me that learning the ABCs at school had once caused him the same difficulty; the basis of communication, like the breath of the hour of Creation, the miracle of being alive, the respiration the neglect of whose observance means disobedience to the primeval law and is the only sin against God the Father! – Death! – "It moved. . . ." Still invisibly, now quite distinctly, its antennae dreamily tasted first of all the pink of the sap of the rose. We looked at each other, Klaus and I, hesitantly eye to eye for a miraculous moment, may he always remember it. I breathed a long, warm breath over my creation of a butterfly, a breath that was still needed to bring it to life. I had already loved the yellow conjurer passionately as a child, had played with it flying through the air, wherever I caught sight of it. After all, it was an image of me, and today it was the precursive miracle of the Judgment Day when, through the patience of God, we will be awakened to life again by him on the blue table of eternity. Suddenly our butterfly got up – his wings began to unfold, he tested them, two magnificent yellow veils; he was one of the brimstone butterflies – he rose up as lightly as a breath, my breath hovered . . . sacred, blessed . . . higher already than a large, consecrated candle over the white Communion, truly straight as a ray of light to the golden birthday – our butterfly – into heaven.

OUTSIDE

Sometimes I look outside into the little garden courtyard. The trees must freeze terribly. They have long since worn out their green and colorfully shaded clothes of leaves, blossoms, and berries, which lie in the junkroom under the snow, rotted in the earth. But why do at least the grown-up trees not take care of themselves, they aren't children anymore; but the tallest giant of a tree is unable to cope with cold and stormy weather, even though the rain and the wafting of the wind are so refreshing and purifying for him, and the rays of the sun so calming. That is why I love the trees that are stripped of their leaves as much as I do those that are clothed. The black, brown-stemmed, large and small trees, and the shrubs and bushes too, exactly as I love my favorite people, from whom autumn is unable to shake the clothes from their bodies, although that would be a welcome development! Since Aunt

Nature with her wealth provides a thousand times richer costumes every year for the oak, the birch, the juniper tree, the cherry tree, the pear and apple tree, indeed for all trees. People, however, get by on their own, and that is precisely the reason why we live only once in life, without having it replaced by the divine welfare worker.

> If I were planted in the earth,
> I would be a silver ash tree,
> And would look forward immensely
> To May, to May!

It shouldn't be all too difficult for me to communicate with the neighboring trees and the mountain ash shrub in the green language, on account of my good breath-beat. Just as the birds' cultivated lungs stand them in good stead when they want to communicate in the botanical language, which is not conducted like the usual languages with the ear and the mouth but is inhaled from tree to shrub, from leaf to flower, and the answer is usually exhaled. That is really the case! The sparrows are interested in plant Greek, although only to the extent that they can assert themselves on the branch from which they habitually observe my window ledge to see whether it has already been set for them or not. Three trees stand in the garden courtyard in front of my window, three friends who know much more of the world than we people. To rejoice with the sky about the blue times of bliss, but also to respect its gray, unpredictable mood. "But just look, that is paradise 'outside'!" Oh, how poor we are in our security and our freedom in comparison to the smallest tree, the most inconspicuous shrub, the simplest flower, whose roots keep pace with the wide earth and grow together – it is possible to live that way outside and rustle one's leaves! When I have something on my mind, I open my window, no matter how cold it is at the time, and ask the trees for their genuine, powerful advice. Between the fibers of their trunks runs their sense of hearing, and intense breath penetrates through the pores of their leaves out through the universe into eternity. They taste my joys and bitter tears, which have sometimes frozen to hoarfrost and fallen hard on the ground; then my three tree-friends threaten with their arm branches, which otherwise can only be moved to comment by a storm.

HOLY COMMUNION

"It was a table of delicate wood, around which Jesus of Nazareth celebrated Holy Communion with his disciples, handed the overflowing, devout rose of his heart to his friends, gave them with this most intimate, strongest embrace eternal life, prepared a home for them, in fact, served the twelve stern Jews with heaven. Only one had not opened his ambitious soul widely and willingly and was suffocated by so much God."

————————————————————————————————

We told each other that cautiously in a lost corner of the coffee house, and the many noisy, busy people in front of us did not notice the sun that went through our hearts and darkened their world. We, however, were lifted up from the floor in a state of blessedness, so moved that we were hovering. You, Arib, looked like the young St. Peter, and you, Juniper Karl, like St. Matthew, and little Dr. Silber, a joyous disciple – and I, who was I, who even as a child was knocking at the great secret of this hour of Holy Communion? The yellow, bitter hops drink in your glass, Arib, changed into gently glowing blood. You lifted the cup to your hard lips and drank, then handed the roselike blood of God to our beloved playmate; he drank. From him with affection St. Silber received the blessed glass and drank. And I, Arib, took the huge goblet from your

66

trusting hand, and I was smiling like a playing brook at noon of the Holy Communion and drank a sea of comfort and trembling oneness with you in God and of eternal life. To us, the miracle was revealed, the beating of wings that opens every door and heals the air of leprosy. Twelve people prepare themselves again and again on earth out of love and fulfill the love. They are the great, unsophisticated Jewish disciples of the Son of God, who climbed down to earth with humble steps from the blue mountain of heaven to tell people that they should love each other. One of his apostles was St. Judas Iscariot. He atoned for his sins by dying on the tree. But one should be on one's guard against the trace of his lips on the edge of the cup of God, from which he drank his wine of the holiest rabbi. It poisons the heart with betrayal. – One of us, my lost playmates, one of us four apostles, one unsuspectingly touched this path of the living glass in the devotion of drinking. I will take the monstrous act without arguing, for the sake of love, upon myself. Disowned, I nevertheless celebrate every evening with you in thought, the little Holy Communion at the round wooden table, the prayer of the most Reverend blood, the festival of eternal life:

Not the dead calmness –
I am already rested after one quiet night.
Oh, I breathe out sleep,
Still rocking the moon
Between my lips.

Not the sleep of death –
Just to speak with you, in heavenly concert
Is rest for me.
And new life begins to sound
In my heart.

Not the black step of survivors! –
Crushed slumbers shatter the morning.
Behind clouds, veiled stars
Hidden over noon –
Thus we find ourselves again anew.

In my parents' house now
Lives the Angel Gabriel
I would like to speak intimately with you in tongues,
To celebrate divine rest in a festival
Love mixes with our words.

Out of manifold leave-takings
Arise, snuggled together, the golden threads of dust,
And not a day passes unsweetened
Between the wistful kiss
And reunion.

Not the dead calmness.
I love so to be in the breath of God.
– on earth with you already in heaven –
Painting on a blue background in every hue
Eternal life.

THE MOUNTAIN ASH

If I possessed a piece of land, I would plant a small forest of
mountain ash trees for myself. Just a single one of the glowing
trees could make and transfigure the happiness of a late summer. Yes, the mountain ash is radiant right into December,
getting daily a little darker and letting its branches droop.
Until the last coral on the umbel waits for the blackbird that
will peck it up. Looking elegant in its black tails, even more
distinguished than the crow, it alights for its repast of red ber-

ries. Often it swings down out of a cloud of snow, and three, four, five, and even more of the black winter guests collect on the hospitable tree. They have it in for that specific tree! From the gardens of the surrounding area a few mountain ash trees still do rise crowned with corals over the roofs of the houses, but the gourmets are keen on dining on precisely our tree. I am their servant and bring dessert: bread crumbs, though on Sundays and holidays I present the charming blackbirds with the sweetest snails. Not live snails in snail-shells, but snails baked from wheat, strewn with currants and glazed with sugar. How blissful, to own an entire little forest of mountain ash, of flaming trees, of branches on which the living coral grows. Black birds come and complete the play of colors! They often approach me as in a fairy tale through fallen leaves or leap up like the wind with the wind!

It took a little while until they knew me and regarded me as one of their own winged souls. I am a blackbird, step on velvet claws through the small door of our dear hotel into the garden courtyard. I myself would be startled if someone unexpectedly decided to bother me with something of no consequence. Because I so like to sit lost in thought between the magnificent birds on the chivalrous mountain ash. It is in reality a female knight, as evidenced by its proud red drops of blood. They don't even need to hide themselves from nature in the veins, they hang in countless umbels on all its multi-faceted branches. When the first snow fell and also clothed the mountain ash, a great big blackbird came, and I saw how it used its pointed beak to free the berries on the tree from the white wet stuff or the moist white stuff. It shook each one of the little fruits of the umbel vigorously back and forth as it saw fit and according to taste, until it considered them cleaned for the table. The black friends, male and female, followed the lively behavior of the diligent worker with shining pairs of

eyes. However, I unfortunately did not notice them magnani-
mously letting it have the few still entirely fresh berries as a
reward for the strenuous work of shoveling snow. But they
themselves feasted, as their pointed beaks drank the wine
from each of the little vines. So very delicately, like the wine
connoisseur, they pushed, at first tentatively, their delightful,
intelligent heads into their feathered backs, tasted and tasted,
before they actually did the honor of swallowing. "Your
health!" I thought. But they don't pay any attention to me
anymore. And no one in the houses round about, in the many
rooms and garrets, has even the slightest idea that it is I who
on Sundays and holidays lets manna, manna with currants
and icing, rain down on the canvas of the summerhouse. Over
it hang the bubbling red branches of the mountain ash.

CITY, BOOK, AND STORES

I write so seldom about books or cities through which I stroll
and that invite me to stay. Books mean cities for me, cities
books, empty and rich with life. And since the book can open
out an entire city for me, with streets and stores and people
who stand in front of their display windows, the bookseller's
lexicon with the announcement of recent publications is
enough for me. Just like the city, so too the book often causes
me to linger, to roam through all its manifold pages. It is not
trade alone that lures people into the big city, or even the
many different entertainments, but the mighty breath-beat,
the tremendous possibility of movement, the exchange of the
exciting illusion of its pulsating thoughts and feelings. Just as
every city is a giant playroom to a Gulliver, even the most
academic book contains its author's toys. He puts them on
show in print. But it doesn't follow for every book that it deals

with the author's grown-up, mature toys; often, unfortunately, it deals only with whitewashed, backward ones. That is why especially the distinguished authors are enthusiastic about the still authentic, simple childlikeness of the folk song. A vision of the heart of sacred gifts. The store is something between the city and the book. Basically, every store is a playroom. Its display window, the big peephole, its playfully embellished welcome. Never, as long as we live, will the play of thoughts and feelings cease, and the blood-red play-chamber of the heart no doubt held the very first game. And already the communicating one – lays out, spreads out his belongings. In a book, though, the person writing it makes a great effort to combine the things and nothings methodically. There is also no price on each of his words, so he demands for his dedication – understanding. He places his production, sometimes also the production from another source of supply, advertised in bookseller's German, on the playground of the market. Yes, toys are probably the main things in the world, the comprehensible and the untouchable. It isn't the royalties, which one for the most part doesn't even receive. It is the tide of talent that hurls the mussels and corals over the brim of our lips. The employed agent of the toy stores of our toys is the publisher   we just get the ideas. For me, even as a child, each book, whether it was about Max and Moritz or about shock-headed Peter, meant a playroom, like every store of our city. And even though I now have so little time, I stop in front of store windows everywhere to look at the many things. I seldom wish to purchase this or that, because – I already have it, having seen it. And just as it is nice now and then to read a lightweight adventure story or romance, I also love to turn over the pages of the most unpretentious store windows of simple stores. The chain stores that sell soap are so amusing, waterbirds, a swarm of them in every district:

Rose, carnation soaps, white and purple lilac
Lie in clean boxes ready for washing again and again.
Between kitschy odors and lavender
All kinds of things are packed
To help the window-shopper pass the time.
At Eastertime
Easter bunnies that produce lather are not expensive.
Brooms, scouring cloths, "sweet scent" for Aunt Meier,
Paintbrushes with and without handles
And beside them the detergents Lux and Persil
Soda, shoe-polish, almost much too much.
All the simple things are knickknacks to me.
I go on my way and I sing:

"There are so many stores, why do I need a bookcase!" Entertainment is provided by the multifarious life of the streets. On top of that, I inherited a playful nature without equal; probably I was born only so that my father could use me as a pretext, pushing me forward so that he, with his white hair, could still inconspicuously look at the toys in the stores. He bought himself spinning tops, marbles, and metal ducks that could waddle and cackle, to amuse himself during his morning snack. But he likewise at the wine merchants', with cries of delight, set the bottles and little kegs of Mosel dancing, his tipsy Punch and Judy dolls. The happy drinkers there were used to him. If one could organize the stores on shelves like books, or put them on marble somewhere, then one would speak of them and differentiate between them as one does with books. There would be novel stores and poetry stores, valuable and deep stores, lightweight adventure and romance stores, and trashy stores. Yesterday, it was on Sunday, a lyrical store, a first-class one, was sent to my house, between rustling silver covers: one hundred years of Friedländer Brothers. The

senior partner of the luxuriously decorated play-store Under
the Lindens himself once dug up the material for the noble
toys – in Australia.

ST. PETER HILLE

Once again I am delighted to write about our dear prophet St.
Peter Hille. All prophets were great poets, as was Peter Hille –
each thought a king! The psalms of David sounded ceremonial to his ear; he spoke of Moses powerfully and respectfully,
of all the prophets of the Holy Land. He decorated the sky-
blue Communion table wonderfully with glowing words.
Prophets were poets; poetry is the blossom of truth. Clearly
and transparently, the poet attains perfection in the state of
inspiration. "Make room for God!" Also, Peter Hille (Petron)
did not like "the half-hearted," the dead, the already stillborn.
Peter Hille's divine model expressed himself even less senti-
mentally and even more removed from the bourgeois men-
tality when he said to one who was later one of his twelve
apostles: "Let the dead bury the dead." Neither of them was
bourgeois – I report with all reverence. The only reason why
Peter Hille did not care about appearances was that he had so
much to organize and to distribute in the world. He himself
was unaware of this, at least he never sought to shine with his
mission. It was precisely his plantlike obedience that proved
he was a prophet. I must always proclaim: he was a star, who
emitted meteors. His life was one of giving; he could not do
otherwise, wherever he turned, than shine on people; naturally in *the* degree to which they looked up to him. Thus, he
carried out the world order, and it carried itself out in him. He
looked after people, that is exactly what was great about him,
that he did not rule people, but looked after them. To have
lived without seeing him is to have missed a creation of cre-

ation. Everyone will confirm that who met him. Peter Hille would have been a pope – to all the world. Because he would have shone on all the peoples to the same extent. A cosmic policy, to be sure, but the higher justice. Peter Hille was intelligent! The thought make me proud. The citizens justified his external poverty (because to be intelligent does not necessarily mean to be practical) by calling him a child. This making a child of someone is just as mysterious to me as making an angel of someone – like giving with one hand and taking with the other. However, people are more inclined to regard watered-down Messiahs or ascetics with snapped wings as "wise men." You see, I am right in the divine picture and capable of distinguishing a sparkling gesture from forced poses. I know perfectly well that we are all God's children on earth, even those who turned out badly. I speak brazenly in the name of Peter Hille when I proclaim that he had fully grown out of the childhood years, physically, but also intellectually and psychologically. The world has not yet stopped confusing what it is to be a child with what it is to be honorable. Peter Hille was truly innocent, and only on this wide, bright slope of his soul did the Highest One plant a new wine of honor. We found his word heavy and fiery, but the flower raised us up mildly and lightly. Peter Hille loved his playmates, just as we loved him, with all ardor. He loved in us, divinely, our capacity to play; his eyes laughed brown and blue in the peace of his face. Certainly he himself had retained the understanding of childlike play as no other.

PETER HILLE

Died the 7th of May 1904

I wrote an entire book about Peter Hille and many other things and once an essay entitled: "Why was Peter Hille invisible?" Did I succeed in revealing to the readers his divine quality? Almost everyone believes only what he sees with his eye, hears with his ear, and mistrusts the feeling of his heart. Only for a few does a strong, trusting nerve herald hours lost in reverie. Never did I doubt the prophecy of Peter Hille.

He strolled over our earth like mist, through which, when it lifted, one saw the stars shining during the day. Of course, he himself was a star who emitted meteors! It is still a part of native tragedy that the prophet is not properly recognized in his homeland. At least not while he is alive. One gets accustomed – even to the miracles that holy people perform. The greatest of miracles, which was accomplished just by the presence of the chosen person – "Peace" – hardly came to the awareness of the neighborhood. Peter Hille was one of the selected guests of this world; wherever his heart turned, unevennesses became smoother. His presence contained reconciliation. A far more powerful, more encompassing miracle than the limited miracle. That is why Jesus, methinks, refused to perform temporal miracles at the wedding at Cana. Toll, which the saint has to pay to prove his worth. – I loved it when the people, even his friends, as I did, remained in front of Peter Hille on a marble step. The affectionate poet Peter Baum and I crowned him with a wreath. Gerhart Hauptmann beamed like a boy who had been given a present; when Peter Hille visited him, Christmas stepped into his room. – Peter Hille didn't say much, but a single word from his lips sufficed to tell a whole story, it was a prophecy, a blessing, a poem, a fiery rose, but also a storm, a summer, an entirely blue sky. His fellow human beings are in the habit of calling the greater fellow human being simply "a child"! They do this comfortably and gladly because they are baffled by him, and prefer to see themselves wrongly as the wise ones. But the children, not yet fixed in their ideas, let their little shovels and pails fall into the sand on the playgrounds when they saw the great man of the clouds approach: the archetypal child. When he smiled, though, all their dear little faces glowed, as did even the big face of the sun up in the sky. *He has already stood before God.* This time on earth he went through his last incarnation. Peter Hille believed that the soul would now and then be put in a body for the purpose of perfecting itself there in that house. He loved his brothers, the prophets. He spoke intimately of Jesus, and decorated the sky-blue Communion table with flowers. He often told me also of the wisdom of Buddha; one could have taken him himself for an Indian, in accordance with the nature of his high unity of movement; he rested in himself like nirvana. "What is that?" And not: "Who is that?" asked the people who saw him.

ST. PETER HILLE

Recently someone asked me what justifies my considering Peter Hille a prophet. For those who know *about* Peter Hille, my answer will be an explanation, perhaps a psalm. It is no fantasy when I maintain that Peter Hille was one of the greatest winged figures of the prophets, who walked on earth again after years and years. In my Peter Hille book, in which I celebrate him in legends, I searched devoutly for his reverent biblical name, and wrote at the conclusion in the book's white earth: he is called what the world is called. Doubtless, I meant the name "Eternity." At that time, when I met Peter Hille, I was, as one says, still very small, sky-blue. Admittedly, he thought I was red and green, and called me: Tino, the little girl with the boy's eyes. That I had already been married, well, who thought of looking into that. I wore a smock, and went into raptures about things, especially about the poet Peter

Baum, who used to recite the "Bridal Soul," the Song of Peter Hille, with enthusiastic love. I know of no one in the world, not even a petit bourgeois, who would not remain humbly before Saint Peter Hille as before the steps of a magnificent monument. But he would not notice at all that he was being observed. He lived in himself as already in God, and going between us, he often strolled as if in a distant, transfigured landscape, illuminating our path, to be sure, but as distant as the moon. – His coat about to fall into dust and he wore it like an ermine, the shoe around his foot worn out: splendor enveloped in ashes. Suspecting who he was, many a person who met us on our trek hurried back to our high companion to stroke the hem of his coat. It comforts me that it was my brother Moriz Maximilian who, shaken by the celestial apparition, gave up the pleasures of the big city and wandered about in the hope of seeing Peter Hille again. In the narrow streets through which Petron and I so liked to walk, the unkempt children gazed at him in wonder: the sparkling St. Martin. His countenance twinkled so. Once I experienced how a bigger street-boy, when he saw Peter Hille, had not just his mouth but also his heart stand still. He approached shyly and – offered the "dear God" his big glass marble, pointing especially to the silver fawn in the little glass ball. "His gala marble," said the smiling prophet, and was very pleased about the present that took him so by surprise. Peter Hille carried the breath of God with him, who not only created him in his image, but also gave him his magic. My landlady, a full-figured woman in pleasing sobriety, who opened the door when Peter Hille wanted to visit me but did not find me in, received me when I returned home with the words: "A man from the Testament was here. . . ." In order to determine whether it was perhaps Peter's beard that brought the woman to that conclusion, I asked her if the man had worn a beard?

She replied *that she didn't know....* Then always, when Petron used to seek me out in the afternoons for sweet cream, bread, and honey, my landlady kneeled before His Majesty in holy awe. "You arch-rascal," threatened my wonderful guest, "what have you been up to again!" Yes, he was without arrogance or false priesthood, pomposity or unctuous tones. He detested every pose; he had no gaps that he would have plugged with the glue of kitsch, and he was nauseated by the fake followers of Goethe who take themselves so seriously as writers. When his *Walther von der Vogelweide* was performed at an outdoor theater, we happy playmates around Peter Hille experienced how he, the blessed one, the celebrated author, happily approached his première coming along the forest path accompanied by a crowd of schoolboys and red caps. Present at the time were the poets of all the arts and a quarter of the inhabitants of Berlin. Peter Hille particularly loved Detlev Liliencron, but also Leistikow, and Julius and Heinrich Hart, the two marvelous brothers, who for one thing didn't carry on like schoolmasters. Was not he himself the main character in his drama: The Platonist's Apostate Son. In the last years of his life, Petron spoke much of Jean Paul with admiration. One would find him in his little room on Kessel Street in Berlin, sitting on the old-fashioned red plush sofa absorbed in a book by the late author. Under his feet rustled torn manuscripts and revisions. White leaves with black veins. He didn't let himself be disturbed in his devotions by anyone who came in, and yet never forgot to let his natural hospitality prevail. Basically, he had no home, his home was where he was looking at the moment, or where he happened to be. And we, his favorites, if we wanted to be with him, we always went to the rock (Petron). He was never sentimental, we felt his mood: by instinct. Peter Hille, the prophet who wrote poetry, was like the horizon. I would hardly know how

78

to describe his prominent *human* characteristics. *Everything* about him was evenly placed, no star shone forth particularly out of his virtues, as out of a bouquet. One or another would perhaps have been presumptuous sometime in daring to call Peter Hille an egoist, despite his great privations; especially since it never occurred to the elemental person to make customary sacrifices. He constantly gave off light, extravagantly, an entire solar system. He didn't even suspect that anyone wanted him to be a cozy little lamb. That's how it is with our great prophets. One should not compare him with those barefoot odious ascetics, who recite their little volume of poetry: Golden Lyre for the edification of anyone they meet. Please, do not try any experiments with him, who may be equated only with prophets and gods. With him, I would also not like to maintain that gods are only representations of great symbols. He was a prophet, the embodiment of a soul as blissful as for a wedding. Music of the marriage with eternity streamed even over the suffering of his life. He strolled on earth in his last incarnation. He had reached the peak. That is to say: he will return to God immediately after his death. His gaze seldom touched anyone's face: *as* one looked up to him, so he shone on the person looking up. I have written an entire book: legends of my Divine Companion: *The Peter Hille Book.* Also several short stories. Today, however, I feel I must give an unembellished answer to the question: *Why was Peter Hille a prophet?* As he did, I love the clarity of imagination, clarification of thought is just putting it into words. No greater diplomat than he could have been found in the Empire during his lifetime; that is to say: if Peter Hille had only possessed the unscrupulous heart in addition! . . . How the people are wrong about their poets and prophets, again and again in every century. St. Petron was a pope. His golden Vatican not of this world. That I of all people, a most fervent Hebrew, draw your attention to Peter Hille, the Roman Catholic, proves that there is only one faith, as there is only one God, one creation, one heaven. Religion, heir to many names and babbling pagan names, is simply accustomed to dressing differently. Thus, one rests in St. Petron's blue words about the Heavenly Son as in Buddha's wise tranquillity, but also in the lap of Abraham! He loved it when I told of Jehovah's great solitude, and dedicated psalms to Zebaoth. In his literary work *The Life of Christ*, Peter Hille adorned the Communion table with the flowers of Nazareth. Now and then, to report honestly, Petron particularly liked to dress like Noah, who tended the vine – and Petron did this *excellently*; like Noah, he drank with great solemn joy the red heart-blood of the grapevine, "the trickling sun" (word-for-word) of the bright berry. – He also performed miracles, by awakening the past in his friend and attracting the coming morning. For all the loving-kindness he was constantly radiating, I nevertheless knew people who had much more human kindness than he did. He was simply a spirit, already almost freed from the body. The most abstract person who walked on earth at the time. So abstract, in fact, that I never remembered when he had left, and hardly remembered when he arrived every evening at my house. He had brown eyes that seemed blue, sometimes full of fantasy. I saw them sing lustily, though, when he came back to the city after a green trek with his Reverend Father Brother Professor Philipp Hille. But when a threatening storm rose up from his Petron heart, his golden-brown domes grew dark. He was no child, as the bourgeois briefly and succinctly like to call him and indeed *every* poet. He was utterly resplendent. Only such a mature presence could dissolve into invisibility. He walked or he hovered. He was deeply shocking in his touching gesture, to be sure; he was a one-thousand-and-two-year-old child, older even than the fairy tales; he had grown for centuries. It wasn't that people held him, but that he held people who *would be great* in the leading-reins of his time. I never heard Peter Hille laugh out loud and yet saw him behave in a Bacchanalian fashion in his circle of friends, a Bacchus, we celebrated him like pagans. He loved joy and celebrations – and he simply *could* not dance. – He spoke almost all languages or all languages. In Sanskrit he found jewels. With gypsies he conversed in the language of their black goddess Bowaneh. St. Petron took his seat in the cart on the box beside Misco, and I had a funny ride through the woods. Peter Hille knew how to answer everything. Usually briefly, he liked to be quiet. When the name Peter Hille is mentioned, why is it that everyone asks: "Who was he really?" Name is no coincidence. The cabalists knew how to draw the root out of the name. So the name of every asker would be his calculation, his balance sheet, his synopsis. Each letter has its number of its outline, the number of its letter. I heard from an expert on the Bible that "64" at the same time means *heart,* so it is allied with him. It is the number I have been encountering ever since I was a child in all sorts of variations, 64 or 46 etc. The heart, certainly, always played a leading role in my life. When I was very young, I caused my mother boundless concern when I saw it hanging dark red on the doorpost of my playroom for seconds. An uncanny symbol. The second time I encountered my own heart was at the gateway through which the prophet St. Petron walked, through the little garden at whose entrance we beheld each other for the first time. I am not going to get worked up telling about him. Getting worked up is what journalists do. St. Petron was silent like the sea, like the rock, and yet answered every question that was directed to him. He was actually the conscience, his soft voice the sound of the world. And his soul was polished to a finish by the tools of humanity, by the human characteristics. If he turned to go, it became dark. If he came, it was dawn. Petron was that related to the earth and interwoven with Creation. – The magnificent, kind Grand Priest and poet Karl Sonnenschein smiled when I told him that was why Peter Hille did not despise worldly beauty, and I often assured him that his coat clothed him like the starry mantle clothed the earth. And I, who still long to give presents to my high friend in heaven, request his canonization on earth. In the years of his youth, Peter Hille wandered barefoot to Rome, and Pope Leo later sent his friend a poem that he, His Holiness, had composed himself and written down in Latin. As long as people live on earth, Peter Hille will never be forgotten, only the dying milieu draws him with it into the grave again and again, as it does with every prophet. The prophet is without honor in his own country, be that in the Orient or the Occident. As people were letting him go hungry and freeze, he in whom poverty and hardship actually ate the deepest, he attained his splendid courteousness. He practiced tact and grandeur, a knight. – He called his quiet, beautiful mother "campanula" or bellflower. In the last year of his life, three loving siblings accommodated him in their large house, the poet Peter Baum, his sister Julia the painter, and their brother Grimmer. When we then grouped ourselves around Petron in the little park, and built him a throne of branches and leaves and pink hawthorn, he looked down at us now and then from his table: "There you exuberant heathens have your Baal!" In *reality* he resembled Michelangelo's Moses. – But Dürer also painted him clairvoyantly, before Saint Peter Hille saw the light – the *light* of the world. Between palms and almond trees, a crowd hurries along behind the prophet, dwarflike behind a holy Gulliver. There is no picture, no photograph that so resembles and catches St. Peter Hille as the picture by the doyen Dürer. He was a miracle, Peter Hille was, and a miracle is not bound by time. I know only of his presence, which redeemed, and of his righteous wrath, which purified. And today I am not just writing his name on the sheet of paper, I am branding it in the skin of all foreheads: he is called what the world is called, *Eternity!*

THE LAST DAY OF SCHOOL

Only for Children Over Five Years Old

To my dear Mama

. . . because people go to school when they are six. Some children are unable to sleep the night before for anticipation, others feel numb: their first playtime is over. No child escapes his school fate, and it comforts him over all the long, long years that it's just the way things are, that all children have to go to school. So the morning comes when one is brought to school. The little girls in their Sunday dresses, the little boys in their new sailor suits to celebrate the memorable day. Soon they can all read, write, and do arithmetic. I have quite detailed memories of these things, not so much of the last day of school, because – I skipped it. And the other school days, too, have almost all healed over in my memory. One isn't exactly too eager to think of them!! But I haven't yet entirely overcome the horrors of school; how often at night my school principal, Mr. Chimney, has appeared to me in a dream as a real chimney in a frock coat, and I think I'm going to suffocate in smoke and soot. That is called nightmares, and it is no fun to dream that way. You see, Principal Chimney always used to come to inspect the class so unexpectedly, with his tobacco pipe in his mouth. The arithmetic problems that I had finally understood fell back down into my stomach, and I gulped and sobbed and had to stand in the corner. At that time, my heart was still a fresh heart-cherry, and *that* was the problem, school always made me conscious of the cherry stone. I look with wistful nostalgia at all children who carry a schoolbag on their backs. It may be different now, after all the schoolchildren went on strike. It was my father who attempted, even back then, to incite me and my eight-year-old girlfriends to revolt against the strict school authorities, telling us that we knew *much* more than the teachers! – As a result, I and Martha Schmidt and Emmy Bachmann resisted going to school. And I remember that my father and I got no cake after lunch on Sunday as a punishment. He claimed he hadn't said anything to us, because he loved to eat walnut cake, and he wailed until my oldest sister secretly put a large piece wrapped in a large paper in his coat pocket. I saw it. – School must be, one has to go to school, how else is one supposed to learn the necessary things for life that one needs in order to make oneself under-stood; I ask you, how? For example, if one goes someday to visit an aunt or an uncle – and wants to write home. One simply *has* to learn how to write! – Or, you see the little books about Indians on the newsstand. The picture on the cover just isn't enough by itself. One simply *has* to learn how to read! If only I had paid better attention in arithmetic; every business-man who publishes my picture-books knows how to pull out the root – ruthlessly, *indeed, from every page!* When one is six years old, the brain is still soft (with not a trace of mortar), letters and numerals impress themselves easily and deeply in the yielding brain mass, like the customary fish form in the warm corn-flour pudding dough. I once saw the brain of a white sugar mouse. It shouldn't be boring for me to tell about it. Mouse-schoolchildren's lessons begin with arithmetic, with mathematics, because of voracity and scraps of food leftovers that fall under the table. The children are usually taught their school lessons by their own mother. "It was winter," said the nice doctor who loved to invite me to visit him, "It was winter," he repeated and made a gesture as if he were freezing; "It was winter and the old Mouse Gray and her little mouse moved into my heated apartment. She gnawed herself a little mouse chamber behind the cupboard, between the molding and the floor, and I sometimes heard her piping voice when her little first-year pupil didn't want to pay attention properly." From every meal that the nice doctor ate, the mouse mother and child boarders received their portion. The food seemed to taste good to both of them; in a quite familiar way they were already venturing out almost to the armchair in which the nice doctor used to rest after the noon meal. Until he set a mousetrap in the twilight; from the tiny gallows hung a small browned piece of bacon; the smell of it rejoiced a long time in his nose. When he was bending down, the nice doctor banged his shiny bald head on the long-legged old cupboard, so that he wobbled like the creaking furniture. That serves him right, I thought; because I found the nice doctor's behavior just as cruel as deceitful. Otherwise had he a good heart? "One catches mice with bacon, my daughter," and then he instructed me and raised his long doctor finger – that I didn't understand all that yet and couldn't judge, but had to be still as a mouse. I confess, however, to my shame, I myself could not wait for the agreeable aroma of the moment that overwhelmed the little mouse in the middle of her cramming for mathematics and compelled her to act. And it wasn't long before the tiny candidate slipped away from her comfortable rectangle, ran in a horizontal line over the nice doctor's new carpet, drew a zigzag square with rapid runner's feet, suddenly hurried through the door – bang!! into the tiny prison. She and the mother mouse teacher had assumed the nice doctor had gone to bed; because before the procedure, I forgot to mention, he had turned out the gas light and lit the petroleum lamp, even placing the green collar around it. At the hour of her death, the little mouse was supposed to be writing her exam. To date, she had only passed the orals, even if she had already brought many a bread crumb, some currants (the nice doctor liked to eat currant bread), and once even a juniper thrush's neck into the dwelling, for which she received a very good mark. The fabulous smell of bacon intoxicated the ambitious young mouse and led to her daredevil exploit. "You see, my daughter," said the nice doctor smiling to himself, "now let's get to work quickly." He held a somewhat roomier cage up to the glass before the opening of the tiny cell, carefully opened the little gate, and the prisoner hurried overjoyed, freed, but only – from the frying pan into the fire. To be sure, she did have a piece of the delicious bacon in her little mouth. "She must have something for her effort," the nice doctor consoled me, holding the glass casket with the gray jewel triumphantly in his hand. For the nice doctor, the mouse was a jewel, and he walked with it into his laboratory, waving to me to come along, certainly to prove its value to me. I hid my face in my small child's hands – I had followed him all the same out of curiosity, and listened through the glittering reddish spaces between my ten pretty fingers, as the nice doctor, a peephole with a gleaming window in it in front of his eye, used tweezers to take the poor mouse's brain out of its head. Then I saw how soft and pliable a young brain is, and the nice doctor showed me seriously as if speaking to a colleague the tiny, wrinkled, reddish-gray mass and lectured: "It doesn't seem possible that so small a world is capable of grasping the large, large world – and – just think, gentlemen, how it is with a young human brain that, aglow with yearning, is capable of exploring not just the splendor of the earth but also the starry heaven, the sun of the day, indeed – the secrets, even the – invisible ones, and ultimately, the Godhead." But that was already too learned for me. I couldn't take any more of it for laughter, my cheeks were threatening to burst, and the nice doctor didn't even notice yet – he was so far, far away. And I made myself scarce. I laughed loudly all the way home; I ran through the narrow streets and even ran quickly up some steps once to look into a garden. On the lawn stood Queen Louise, although some of the children maintained it was Flora of Athens. There were also beautiful blue and pink forget-me-nots in the flower beds, my favorite flowers. – But I still had to do my school assignments. I didn't feel like doing them at all. It was always particularly difficult for me to write essays. For my essay on "Frederick the Great" I had received a failing grade, and for "Winter in the Sudeten Mountains" my oldest sister, who had just returned from boarding school, was going to help me. My greatest fear was of getting a detention, it was so boring alone in the classroom. Outside in the Wupper River the workers were rinsing the dyed cotton. That was why, it occurred to me, the dear river always shimmered like black milk that had gone sour. Then I fell asleep. I did prefer the lessons to staying in. We often played that we were in a café, especially in the geography class. None of us cared a bit where the other cities lay, and I was only interested in the African rivers because they rhymed. And they flowed like water from my lips: Senegal and Gambia, Niger or Dcholiba, Zaire and Orange River, Nile and Zambesi. With this poem I earned my first and only praise. I wrote it into the class register in school and preserved it forever. Miss Kreft was also the only teacher who believed in me. Always, when she had something memorable to say, she put a piece of licorice in her mouth first, like the time she expressed her opinion of me to our dear mama: "Else is basically not all that stupid." Actually, Papa was to blame for everything, since he was the one who bought me the candies and the chocolate that prevented me from paying attention in class. He was so very sorry afterwards, when he had scolded me, and I was clever enough to provoke him on many occasions. Together with us children, he was secretly furious with our arithmetic teacher Mr. Gramm. Before we even reached the school gate he would divert me and my girlfriends and encourage us to skip the arithmetic class. Then he bought many, many sweets and a quantity of firecrackers; he had immense fun setting them off. One of us sat there in a soldier's cap, the other in a turban, I in a sailor's hat, and my papa in a white cap, around the table in the office; long ribbons trickled down over his ears. Yes, even they were laughing, his entire face surrounded by his white beard, and the smallest white hair on his head laughed. He was dressed like such a young person, and when he told us about his parents, he was still sitting in their lap or Grandpapa had just given him a beating, because he was the naughtiest of the brothers. When we had had enough to drink and eat, he played with us wild children: schoolmaster. He got the thick pointer out of the corner, and we had to sing the ABCs with him. It went this way – (We:) "a b c d e f g h i j k l m n o p." (Schoolmaster:) "Can't you learn the ABCs, can't you learn the ABCs." (We:) "q r s t u v w x y z." (Schoolmaster:) "I would rather tend pigs than be a schoolmaster, I would rather tend pigs than be a schoolmaster." (We:) "a b c d e f g." (Schoolmaster:) "Multiply, divide, and correct as well." (We:) "h i j k l m n o p q r s t u v w." –In religion, I just about forgot to report, I was a good pupil, the story of Joseph made a deep impression on me. Once I cried so bitterly about the part where Joseph's beautiful velvet coat of many colors was dipped in blood by the brothers that the priest was moved to send me home. As soon as I got home from school – I played cops and robbers with the little boys in our narrow street. Sometimes the Saint Bernard dog came leaping over the fence of the other people's garden that bordered on our little street; beside ourselves with fear, we called as in one voice: "Mama!!" – I also liked to do handi-work. The needlework teacher praised me for my diligence. I knit socks as long as my arm, and the teacher would often ask: "Where will that end!" My sisters used to wrap up all sorts of knickknacks in balls of wool for me. I went through the wool so quickly. Surprise after surprise fell into my lap: a little gold bag, a tiny plate, a little spoon, a small pot, a little sugar bowl – until the little service was together; once a tiny tinkling piano made of porcelain came out. When the right sock was fin-ished, I had lost the left one; it had usually been appropriated by my papa, because, as a way of honoring the memory of the Westfalian farmers, he liked to carry his money in a sock with a number of papers, scribbled full or painted. – My papa got along very well with the English teacher from Leipzig who taught us children the English language. On many occasions he bought "jewelry boxes" for Miss that I had to bring to her. She put them in the cupboard until after class. For that, she didn't ask me too many questions. I learned French as well as I could from my mama, whom I adored. She loved that lan-guage as a way of honoring the memory of the great French emperor. I inherited her enthusiasm for the brilliant and just Basilius, he is still my type today. I am not being indiscreet when I maintain that he was the great love of my mother's life; mementos of "Him" hung under glass in a frame on the wall. Among other things there was a small scrap of material from the sofa on which Bonaparte was born. My dear mother read a lot; books papered the four walls of her little living room. Sometimes it seemed to me at lunch that she was think-ing of some woman or some knight from the novel she was reading. At those times her eyes were opened wide and seemed to see so far, as if to the other end of the world – or high over the water, as in powerful birds who would like to fly far away. Then I always felt so sorry in my heart, I would have liked to sacrifice it for her even at that time, to please her with the small blood-red scrap, in addition to the frayed sofa-relic preserved under glass. In my imagination, the relic grew into a magnificent bed. One day my dear mother went up into the forest. Our house was at the foot of the hill that led into silent green prayer. She didn't come home for the evening meal – there was thunder and lightning from all directions, green, then red from across the sky: purple and now yellow, yellow as a lemon! My papa and all my sisters and brothers went looking for Mama. Oh, it was so sad – when even a child gets lost – but especially as in this case – a mama. . . . My papa was wailing bitterly with his eyes open, like a tiny baby. I took care not to look at him so I wouldn't have to laugh. There was lightning the whole time and then thunder afterwards, how scary! I climbed up into our tower, from which I could look out on all sides. Suddenly I saw my dear, dear mama coming down the little mountain so sadly, so sadly that I cannot describe it. To do so I would have to take my heart out of my breast and teach it to write. But it girded itself in a single drop of blood that knew no danger, and I leaped over the wooden roof terraces of our tower in order to reach my poor mother more quickly; became entangled, however, in the Venetian blind stretched out of the lower window of our tower and lay there as safe as in my mother's arms.

Because all children have a special guardian angel. I was rescued from the parachute by my second brother, who belonged to the volunteer fire department. My brother carried me on his broad shoulders from step to step, from air to air – I had such tremors through my body – down the long, frightening ladder. – I had come down with Saint Vitus' dance. The nice doctor thought it was a result of the fright I had received! From that time on he called me: "lively little kid!" But I knew that I had gotten Saint Vitus' dance from something entirely different – from the first grief in my life, that not even the loveliest parental home had been able to prevent. However, because of that, I didn't have to go to school anymore. "There can be no talk of going to school anymore," said the nice doctor, in a dictatorial tone at that.

IN THE GARDEN COURTYARD

Without offending the cats, who suffer from the callousness of humans

I live almost at the root of the three trees in the garden courtyard, the trees that I have already mentioned several times. I moved down a story into a larger room, but that means I can't have conversations with the trees anymore. Like we do, they naturally have a face and a mouth for speaking. For me, trees are people too, at least creatures that draw breath from the spring water of the air, are thirsty, refresh themselves, can be sad and overjoyed, and are incomparably happy all summer long. On one of the many leafless branches of the linden hangs something silly that has been there since New Year's. That annoys me, it brings disorder in the uncovered branches, in the symmetry of its winter, since not even the snow was able to wash off the faded strips of paper. I would not invite anyone to view my garden courtyard. It is perhaps even more simply planned than each of the garden courtyards in front of the other houses in the neighborhood. It serves exclusively for airing the hotel rooms. People staying at the hotel seldom look out on it from their windows, and they would hardly consider it possible that anyone could be capable of writing a word about our courtyard or the one across from it, let alone writing poetry about them. But anyone who can write poetry can conjure up a paradise from a handful of earth. Today, however, all melancholy has gathered under the three trees. The rooster was roasted, and people made New Year's soup from the hens. Only the hotel cats are still alive. They seem gray to me, creeping mist that would like to settle in the cellar, secretly brooding young that are as blind as eggs. Cats are a miaow unto themselves! I am afraid of cats, not just of their enigmatic eyes, whose mystery has probably been overestimated. Also, I myself am too much a bird not to take sides. Yes, I flee with the flocks of birds from all that is boneless, even from the flattery of the playful young newborn kittens! I am also outraged that the bread crumbs I spread for the starving birds are probably taken by the cat. The birds are my true friends; God knows. It happened in the year just past that someone fired a shot into the garden courtyard from the other side. I was surprised by the clap of thunder in winter that, as it turned out, did not come from the sleeping cloud but from a pistol shot. The tomcat lay slain by a murderous hand on the moist little lawn. From his side streamed a rising red river. I have never seen so much blood in one place. One could have swum to hell in it. Because in the nights he used to rape underage cats, and the spotted Rosa, so the elevator boy told me, was also the victim of his lusts. His indiscreet adventures awakened the tired travelers staying in our hotel and the people across the way. And pardon my saying so, but many a fossilized bachelor envied the tomcat's limitless freedom. I must say, I felt sorry for the tomcat; he had perished. We were happy not to have been hit by the bullet. But I did attempt to overcome my aversion for the cat family. When I came home to my room a few afternoons ago and wanted to open my window, I was surprised by the game two of our hotel cats were playing. They were playing just like schoolchildren: "hide-and-seek!" The yellow one of the four cats hid herself between old junk, a sofa and armchairs, tablecloths and curtains that had been put out to air in the yard, while Rosalinde, the one who had been seduced early in life, waited in front of our garden gate for her playmate's signal from across the way. . . . And then with a leap she sprang over the wooden thicket into the other people's yard, searched their hall and cellar, came back out again; sniffed at the rotten, dusty fabric of the furniture, and finally found her companion with a childlike miaow. Then it was Rosa's turn to look for her friend, and so the game repeated itself continually. Until a simply beautiful, slim crow came flying by, settled on the nearest bare juniper bush, and awakened innocent instincts in the playing cat children. A single red berry still hung on the branch, one coral on the bough. I was intoxicated by the one glowing drop still preserved for me from the summer.

THE ILLUMINATED WINDOW

Even as schoolgirls, my friend and I liked to stand in front of illuminated windows in the evening and make up stories that would never occur to me today. I don't know if all children like to look through bright windows in the twinkling darkness as if through Easter eggs into Fairyland. In any case, it was one of our favorite pastimes, and we conjured up unforgettable dreams behind the glass of the evening hours. Onto the milky-black Wupper of our hometown stare mysterious, dark houses of slate reflected in the black water. These workers' barracks with their peepholes had us bewitched and haunted our senses. My friend's name was Martha Schmidt. Her father was always friendly to us "bosom friends." His beard-framed face always smiled a greeting, even when he complained of hard times. Martha's wise mother was how I imagined Cassandra to be from the world history classes at school. At any

93

rate, Mrs. Schmidt prophesied just as reliably as that daughter of Troy. To the two of us, at least, she predicted everything in advance, when we had raced through our homework together, giggling and looking out the window all the while. Frau "Emily" knew the classics by memory without a hitch, and sometimes she recited to us girls the doyen's [Goethe's] *Iphigenie* or Friedrich von Schiller's "Song of the Bell." Tears ran down our faces from laughter, unnoticed by the woman, who was in a state of ecstasy. Once in her hometown, when she was engrossed in the study of Kotzebue, she fell from the third story of the house to the startled street below, causing malicious newspapers to report about fallen literature. But Martha and I both loved her, she always had a little surprise for us in the drawer of the table, which was supposed to make the way to school more pleasant for us, because school was something terrible for us dreamers, a sentence we innocents were condemned to serve for ten years. For allowing us to escape our sentence for a few days, we have to thank our – by arrangement – easily inflamed tonsils and exaggerated difficulties in swallowing. In the afternoon, we secretly visited each other with our necks wrapped up in scarves; at the time when my relatives were having afternoon coffee, I sneaked out the garden gate, ran by a circuitous route in a big hunchbacked arc over the back of the city to Martha, who was already dressed and waiting for me on the edge of her bed. Mr. Schmidt thought that we had caught cold by all our looking out the window in the chilly evening hours. Sitting between us girls, he took his silver toothpick carefully out of its case and cleaned from his teeth the remains of the delicious apple cake that he had consumed with great gusto. Only I jerked up off the seat of the chair every time he chirped between his teeth and the row of brittle biters behind his lips wobbled. He didn't take the slightest notice of my discomfort; on the contrary, when his daughter nearly died laughing about my nerves, it made him, with all the more friendly understanding for me and his Martha, click gluttonously with an amplified whistle through the gap of his enormously long eyetooth, as if he knew all our secrets and would keep them with us behind his meticulously starched shirtfront. When the big tree in the yard of his house was in its fullest foliage, father Schmidt always regretted not being a little calf. Martha and I, however, used to disappear after the evening meal into her parents' bedroom. From there, leaning shoulder to shoulder, we observed the illuminated window of the house across the street. Behind the silk curtains, in reality a fabric of strong thread, lived an Indian prince, both of us lived for him with our eleven-year-old fairy hearts, both of us invented stories about him, until we were inconsiderately driven apart. Sometimes, though, I stayed overnight at Martha's. Then she lent me one of her nightgowns. She was shorter than I was, and it only came down to my knees, something I was ashamed of each time I appeared in my dreams before the exotic king's son in his splendid robes and turban. Usually, however, my father came for me with his thunderous way of walking, as if an entire squadron marched cursing up the narrow street and planted itself with a fanfare in front of Martha's parents' house. Even if it was the middle of the night, I was mercilessly raised from sweet slumbers to come along home with him! To make up for it, he put my little hand in his big coat pocket, from which I could take out a horseradish candy for myself, or a glass collar-stud, or the colorfully ringed spinning top from his toys. When the Renz Circus arrived in our city with its male and female equestrians, twenty-five huge elephants, fourteen camels, an albino dromedary, a chimpanzee, sixty Arabian horses, zebras, trained lions, a giraffe, clowns, and the outstanding August himself, we forgot about the king's son from

Benares. We admired the advertising posters showing things that had never come to the city before, aquatic acts and elfin ballets. From that time forth, Martha and I visited my father every evening in his office and attempted to persuade him to go to the circus with us. Although he had snow-white hair, we thought of "him" as one of our playmates. After Renz had set up his circus on Brausenwert Square, my father himself could "hardly wait for evening," and he was already waiting impatiently for us two children when it began to get dark. But he always let himself be pressed and pestered by us, and we often climbed after him right up to the roof of his newly built observation tower. We had fallen in love with "Joy Hodgini," at least I had, he was my ideal, my very first true love. On his golden-blond head of curls he had the stiff felt hat pulled casually back from his forehead toward the back of his neck. His black eyes looked languid, and he had a powdered, tired face with English features – that was how he encountered me alone for the first time on King Street. I ran to my girlfriend! Together with her and with the entire grade seven class, who had discovered him a long time ago, we trotted along behind the enchanting jockey, who now and then turned around and graciously blew kisses at us with his slender hands. Just think: black eyes and golden-blond hair! Every day at twelve noon the race began from the schoolyard; and yet – he loved only me – as Martha bravely admitted. From that time on I refused to carry my schoolbag on my back anymore. Instead, I always held upright in my hand a rose in full bloom, a rose from our weeping rosebush for "him," until one day Martha snatched it resolutely from my fingers, threw the waiting flower at Joy's feet and said, pointing to me: "from Else Schüler." It was his lovely smile that caused us to call him "dream," so that we could always talk about him inconspicuously. We wily customers had also found out where he lived, and it filled us with pride to be witnesses to the way he tied his red tie in all kinds of variations behind the illuminated moonstone of his window. We promenaded on tiptoe back and forth in front of his house until one time his sister Nelly, the tightrope-walker, together with my oldest brother, who was in love with Joy's sister, appeared at the window and sprayed us two girlfriends with perfume. We smelled of it for days and were identified by it. The third illuminated window, however, was a large arched window in the stairwell that we saw from the stairwell of our hall, looking across our street into someone else's pear orchard. With all kinds of fear, I looked through the mysterious arch, behind which a little old lady was washing the household laundry. But I changed the aged washerwoman into a wondrous rabbi, about whom I wrote a small book just a few years ago, in which the Jews built Him a safe palace whose dome protected Him from trouble. For a quarter of a century this literary work fermented in my heart, became a vineyard, old Spanish wine, a Jewish grapevine as old as the stars. With art it is just like with grape juice. The longer it is allowed to develop in the cellar of the heart, the more potent it becomes. Ever since the arched window had revealed itself to me, I tended to cling to my mother in fear when I was going to bed. With big eyes, I told my dear mother the secret of the illuminated glass, and she said, "You are a poet." Now that she is dead and can no longer partake in person of the table I have set with my verses, my soul grows sad. She is in heaven, and in the redness of the evening sunset I seek her behind the illuminated garnet of the window in the clouds. Night has fallen. One of my friends comes to mind, whom I always looked after with great care; because as children we played marbles in the street, seesawed in the meadows with boards laid crosswise over each other, slipped and slid over frozen streets when the world still lay behind fresh gauze, when there were still illuminated windows. We strolled up to such a wondrous window, tired glass softened by the traffic lights. My companion thought to surprise me with the sight of two of his former school-friends, two Pharaohs. Expectation strengthened our resistance against the strongly armed winter evening. "You won't be sorry that you waited!" my companion said encouragingly. But neither Amenophis nor Tutankhamen emerged from their sarcophagi. The high spirits, though, served up by our wait, we drank from the bowl of the moon. Unfulfilled expectation in front of an illuminated window fortifies the heart and fills it with eternity. Only no policeman is allowed to come, not even a nice one like the policemen of today who are among the gentlemen of the street. The dashing one that night wore a coat of snowflakes, two icicles bent conservatively over his upper lip, and said: "It's winter – haven't you noticed?"

PARADISES

Wherever you look there is still a bit of paradise. Even if you go right past it – only a few people recognize the shimmeringly preserved flower bed of our very first home again. The entire world was once . . . paradise, a glowing melon on the branch of eternity, and fell into God's lap. Until the first human couple was seized with fear, our earthly paradise darkened and lost its equilibrium. Fear darkens, and the loss of balance produces fearful darkness. That is how the still-gentle light in the chalice of the paradise world was extinguished. With hints of blue, the sky hung over the young earth, on which God separated the water from the land. From a handful of earth he created the first man in his own image. Probably everyone at one time has a vision in a dream, or even when awake, of that landscape that he seems to know already. But that landscape itself is not what surprises the dreamer or the wanderer. What always dazzles us is only its perfect paradisal light, which our eye has forgotten how to see, the primal light, the intimate face of our origin. We used to walk through the forest sometimes. Once one of us suddenly collapsed with the cry: "But I was here before this life!! . . ." He almost fell into the little splashing brook on us; it was not a hysterical person who became unconscious, but a skeptic, taken out of the coolest depth of his heart and awakened. He of all people was over-whelmed to the point of being paralyzed by the primal flash of insight. These people get their Weltanschauung from the book-cover of the world. They are the people with the world-view. But the world views us. How unchildlike these learned people actually are with the arrangement of their world. Aren't they? The possibilities, the transformations of time: landscapes of God the Father, come only to him who is recep-tive to them. Let me tell you something. An Indian legend. It may be that it is true. Once upon a time the surly stag beetle noticed a tree standing between other trees; they were actually all the same, and the wind acted as mediator in their conversa-tion with each other. And when the Indian was in the process of stretching himself out on the grass under the branches of the one tree, a flame wound its way over his body, a flame whiter and wiser than he had ever seen before. Then he recog-nized how right his copper-colored girlfriend, "The Decorated Wildfire," was when she said: "There are things about which we have not the faintest idea." As I said, almost every person experiences at some time the vision of paradise. I mean, he recognizes the clear, loving light over our world. All our seed was planted on the sunny slope of the first person, and an en-counter with the bit of paradise means a reunion with home. A remnant of Eden still hangs everywhere, even in the noise of the street. A bright word, a magical leaf, the silver cloud high in the sky, in the jewelry of lovers, in the kiss of the lips along the path of love. The still-bright world was love that had taken shape, the young Godhead himself. We all search for the bit of paradise with the fervor of all our energy. Its darkened light is God's secret. But light is love that cannot be entirely extinguished. Therefore, a ray still hangs everywhere magically, a ray that kisses your foot. The skeptical one should take care that his bit of paradise doesn't shrivel up or become bitter on his scales. Love is not to be weighed.

He who cannot give his paradise to one person will of necessity offer his love to the crowd. So let no one boast to me about his love of the world. Even if the individual person is only a little star of blood, he often represents an entire people. Anyone who wants to learn about paradise should seat himself under the trees; it is possible to tarry under a single paradisal leaf. Its entire branch longs for the light of eternity. I am most obliged to His Reverend Plantship the acorn for his wise insight about paradise: the tiniest life on earth longs to diminish darkness. The fish illuminates the river, the mountain reaches out for the embrace of the blue cloud. Even when it was just an outline, the plan for the world wore the revealing light of love as an *ex libris*. We all search for the bit of paradise, it shelters the perfect radiance of the world of love. We would all like to be lit up like Christmas trees. When even one little light is burning, especially when we are standing right in its glow!! But most people are encamped in the cellar, poor souls!! Even the prostitute longs in her subconscious for the remnant of paradise. Her profession is only a pretext. Love is always a possession of the psyche, sexuality its vessel. So to reject sexuality means to neglect the body that houses the soul. This happens on many occasions through error. But I do think the sexuality that does not seek the paradise of love must be condemned, just like the body that houses its soul inhospitably and lets it fall into disrepair. The romantically inclined virgin, if there are any of them left, should not despise the nocturnal temptress; the latter is basically only pursuing the bit of paradise. I praise the Don Juan who only goes through all the hearts in pursuit of the one paradisal heart! Naturally there is a love, prepared in the love-light of the Holy Land, that does not need the vessel. It emerges in the conversation that turns into a concert. I myself was witness to such a transubstantiation into an angel. Resplendent in the words of the Godhead were the great archangels. The bit of paradise in every nuance of light bequeaths a meaningful trace to what has been revealed. However, the result of our darkened paradise is: nearsightedness to the point of blindness, feuding, the thirst for power, hate and war, and the recognition of love shines wanly in the hearts of humans. But paradise lives, even if secretly, in the hanging traffic lights of the world. Only its unclouded ray can save the world again, only its love can save mankind. "My paradise lives in your eyes." Yes, if we were all making an effort to develop the tiny remaining bit of paradise again, we should soon be playing in paradise. But we people would certainly already have mutually toppled each other if we did not, like stars, have to follow an astrological law. It must be that from the very beginning we have had a jewel to protect, the ruby of the love of paradise! I know friends who suffer from the fear of paradise, a fear that can only arise from the darkening of the world. Dull habit suppresses this primal agony in most people. If the agonized person succeeds in flicking over his page into the present, then the revolt of a little wave of blood from his heart is enough to reopen the yellowed pages of pre-memory. And as it happened in our darkened world, even the person darkened by fear can be thrown off balance. Anyone who has experienced this primal agony knows how the earth suffered when the light of paradise – love! – slipped away from it.

On the Feast of St. Lawrence there was a procession in my hometown. The Roman Catholic schoolchildren had the day off and didn't need to go to school. But they put on white clothes and were – angels, on that day. Angels large and small, from the highest to the lowest grade at school. Usually, the Feast of Saint Lawrence fell on a Sunday, and then we other children had the day off as well, the "Lutheran and Semitic children," as the teacher used to differentiate between us. On this day we could again look on as the Catholic girls we went to school with assembled on the Catholic church square, around the two-spired church behind the rustling chestnut trees. One of the trees blossomed piously, the other always a little tempestuously into late summer, until the solid chestnuts came that now and then fell on the shoulders of the benevolent, smiling chaplain. We paid rapt attention when we played marbles, squatting on the cleaned ground with our glistening marbles. Today, however, there was an entirely different sight to be seen on the Catholic church square, and above all in the streets. The high-school students and those from the vocational schools sat precariously on the housefront arabesques, even on the roofs. My wondrously pretty oldest sister always joined in; I watched her admiringly as she sat up on a slate roof courageously leaning against a chimney beside Julius Caesar, the most intelligent boy in the highest grade. She was jauntily waving a blade of grass between her lips. The little schoolboys almost pushed in the ground-floor windows of the rows of houses with their stubborn backs, sometimes the windows rattled disastrously. Basically, the whole city was involved in the procession, and on the Feast of St. Lawrence the Lutherans seemed to quite like the Catholics; just as they liked us Jews on the Feast of the Passover because of the matzos. All the inhabitants of our city of Elberfeld were on their feet, only Karl Krall came riding by on his "clever Hans," on the back of his horse that could do arithmetic like a mathematics professor.

My papa held me by the hand. He was feeling extremely tense and alert, and breathing heavily like a tempest. "You naughty child!" he reprimanded me, "always having to do wee-wees just when the baldachin is coming." He dove hastily with me behind a fruit basket that had been left behind from market day. The children in the procession all wore wreaths of white roses in their hair, and the grown-up angels had long white veils hanging from their holy faces right down to their feet. Nuns came to the Feast of Saint Lawrence celebrations too, having made the pilgrimage in the morning from the Neviges convent to Elberfeld. The Catholic children announced this to each other by whispering in each other's ears. In my district, the Lutheran religion had become more widespread than the Catholic religion, and there were always arguments between the Lutherans and the Catholics, especially since the Lutheran sect of pietists lived in Wuppertal. But in the end it was always the Jews who suffered, living very much to themselves as the smallest congregation between the Christians. Only ma papa ne'er took no notice a' that. Whene'er it came t'a brawl 'tween the religions, he jus' leaped right in 'n' joined the fight. The children of the pietists had it in for me in particular, because I wore a little red dress. And I always opened my eyes so wide – that made me look so inspired and strange, so exotic . . . certainly stemming from the fact that I was always dreaming about Joseph and his brothers. "Hepp, hepp!" called the Lutheran children until the little Catholic girls imitated them. "Hepp, hepp!" the good, sympathetic chaplain explained to me, just meant "Jerusalem is lost."

Once Jesus Christ had sat in the moon at night; I was asleep, of course, but he came really close to my bed in a dream and said: "Jerusalem is not lost, since it lives in your heart." That strengthened me greatly against the superior strength of my attackers. And once Adele ran after me on the way home. Adele was actually the one most given to yelling insults. But she, of all people, suddenly embraced me, right in the middle of the street, linked arms with me and went with me under my precious little new umbrella through the wet streets. To be sure, she knew I had the little white dress with the flounce of embroidered leaves. No child abused me when I wore it to the Sedan celebration in the assembly hall. Adele was always oh-so-poorly clothed, even in the procession; although she was carrying the children's Holy Heart of Mary on a blue atlas pillow. She once showed me the sacred oil painting with a lot of gold decoration in the front room of their poor apartment. Her father fastened it to the flag on every Feast of St. Law-rence. Adele said to me: "I like you best of all in the class, and I will never yell hepp, hepp again." She had gone to confession, and the chaplain had made her say the rosary many times in penance – and she had to ask my forgiveness. She admitted that to me with her whole heart, with her whole strength and her tear-streamed love and true longing for a girlfriend. Then the two of us hopped through the gate into our little garden, ate from the licorice tree and plucked the few still-unripe hazelnuts. Then I showed Adele our lizard: Caroline. My fa-ther had bought her for me for the grotto of our garden room. And finally, we secretly climbed arm in arm up the many stairs to my bedroom. I dressed Adele in my white dress and she looked wonderful in it. She was very pale and held her arms up all the time away from her thin body so that she wouldn't get any dirt on the dress. I gave her my amber neck-lace, too, and my forget-me-not ring and my chocolate chim-ney sweep and my bright red wineglass as presents. That is why Adele was the most beautiful angel in the procession the next Feast of St. Lawrence, and my father tapped my little hand, just to make sure – he had thought for a moment that I was Adele. She, however, walked majestically and gloriously, blown from the shiny trumpet, between two other Catholic angels, in front of the baldachin in the procession – probably into the kingdom of heaven.

THE INCA BUTTERFLY

My uncle Sebastinos suddenly came back to Europe. Since he has been back again, everything, at least everything in our house, smells of the sea and of tar and of all kinds of foreign plants. From Grandmother's nose, all the time now, hang two wads of cotton wool sprinkled with eau de cologne. But I am refreshed by the extract of the great "great water," as Uncle calls the ocean. Sometimes I swing myself up on his broad knee, on my South American mustang – "Such a big boy!" Who finds anything odd about that? Grandmother, probably – but I have arrived in Uncle Sebastinos' distant world, from which he actually never came home. Best of all, I like to hear about the life of the incomparably magnificent butterflies of the country, of the black Inca butterfly with the green border on its wings, the sacred butterfly of all the Indian tribes. They are fanatical about it; brother kills brother if he can prove that he did harm to the butterfly of the gods. Yes, they are really keen about the black Inca butterfly, and the Indians guard the tea plantations with Indian loyalty. The hovering idol likes to stay in the tea plantations most of the day. And that on account of the tea-rose, who takes her five-o'clock tea punch there from the blossoms of the tea bushes. The tea-rose butterfly doesn't get its name from the golden-brown color of its graceful wings, but because it stays in the area of the Mexican tea fields. Uncle Sebastinos explained it to me in these words: "In particular the love-life of butterflies has something so tender about it that no human can begin to understand it." In order to better tell the story and to be able to spit to his heart's content, Uncle chewed his gum vigorously; I alternated with him in biting pieces off the thick stick; at first I had refused, thinking he was chewing a stick of dye, until I courageously tried some. One day he succeeded in actually capturing an Inca butterfly. "With my bare hand," he emphasized. It formed a loving, cool dome over it – a shadow – being very careful out of respect for the ancient Indian cult. The powerful butterfly had lit on the big lapis lazuli on his finger, and Uncle seized the opportunity that would probably never come again. Uncle Sebastinos' house in Mexico was on tall stilts because of the danger of wild animals in the night and because of the snakes that came winding into the village from the primeval forest at dusk. And it was a poisonous rattlesnake that came again and again and could not be eradicated. It fetched the skins from the sausages that the cowboys received from their sweethearts in the capital city every week to eat for dinner on their way home. Uncle Sebastinos said he was so happy that he actually gave off sparks on the way home with his rare find in the dungeon of his hand. He had always sort of suspected that he would bring such an Inca butterfly home someday. And for that purpose he had prepared an airy accommodation for it, a truly hospitable butterfly palace. The holy prisoner now hovered through its limited expanse. Sometimes, unfortunately, it bounced terribly off the horizons of the sealed-up world and attempted again and again to find a way out. As wild and violent as Uncle appeared, it did pain him deeply to see the Inca butterfly a prisoner, even though he could have freed it instantly. He was also very concerned about the increasing melancholy of his sacred captive. One morning when Uncle was in the process of carpeting the floor of the Inca butterfly's cage with fresh tea leaves, something wondrous happened. Uncle counted at least one hundred and fifty tea-rose butterflies, some of which besieged the portal; others pressed themselves, winged, shimmering flowers of gold, against the front of the Inca butterfly's palace. But much more dangerous rebels had united against him and were stealing around his garden fence, some of each of the most threatening Indian tribes. Pampeia, daughter of the chief of the Pampas, had for a long time secretly observed the golden-brown Amazon army of tea-roses. And she had gotten suspicious. . . . Two transparent glass beads ran down my Uncle Sebastinos' cheeks, but when I looked more closely, they were two big, round tears. For until then Pampeia had flirted with him from the crown of a primeval forest poplar, and he had loved the copper-colored Indian maiden from the bottom of his heart. Oh, it filled him with pain even to talk about it. She, of all people, was the one who betrayed him! It was Pampeia who informed the Pampas where the sacred animal was being kept, and they informed the other Mexican tribes. Sometimes my uncle used to wake up early in the morning with an old Indian folk song about the sacred Inca butterfly and the tea-rose going through his head. My poor uncle. If only I could still repeat the song!! I was bursting with curiosity. Indeed, we were all bursting, because in the meantime all my schoolfriends had come and were sitting on his shoulders; my friend Peter, who was sitting beside me on my uncle's other knee, suddenly raced out and came back in again; with others hanging on to his arms in pairs. He was very deeply affected by the song. He chirped it out brightly again and again, one, two, three times in a row. Suddenly we all felt at once that he was thinking of his flame: Pampeia. Pampeia had betrayed him –

coming home from the plantation, he was climbing up the ladder to his house when he saw her form hurriedly disappear and climb over the fence. She had cut through the silk threads of the walls of the Inca's cage with the knife in her belt. And then my uncle became aware of what wounded him the deepest, his worshiped Inca butterfly was hovering high over the flower and vegetable beds of his garden, accompanied by a golden-brown cloud, an army of tea-roses, and they flew away, away into the wide, wide world of Mexico. "I have never been one to cry," he maintained, "but now I wept bitterly and in my grief did not notice the sting of the poisonous rattlesnake that the chief's daughter, seeking revenge, had secretly wrapped like a vine around the back of the chair I used to sit in to observe the Inca butterfly." Uncle pointed to his left arm which was motionless and rigid. We clasped it like a firm pillar.

THE YOUNG FRIEDRICH NIETZSCHE

When I took the train through Thuringia some time ago, an older lady got into my compartment in Weimar, and I will think of her with gratitude for the rest of my life. She and Friedrich Nietzsche had been friends when they were young. And I would have controlled myself and silently breathed in the naphthalene and the camphor, or breathed in the camphor like naphthalene, if I . . . had even suspected. . . . These smells streamed from the cape from the 1880s that the wife of the retired counselor pulled out of her embroidered traveling bag. As it was, however, I sprayed myself and the woollen antique with lily of the valley, which Dralle had picked daintily in the perfume of his homeland – nevertheless, the charming lady said mockingly, perfume, no matter how good it might be, would always be more open to criticism than a useful chemical; although she did find eau de cologne acceptable. I agreed with her! Because people have to get along with each other on the train. I even love being well-trained on the train. The wife of the retired counselor found my chatter pleasant, which is how it came about that she told me the sweet, heroic story of Friedrich Nietzsche's youth, a story that I now generously pass on to all humanity – having kept it to myself for as long as I promised. How poor, in comparison, is a gift to one's homeland in the form of an endowment or a museum or even castle grounds. With a play of silver in the cold sky, a swarm of birds flew into the wide world along with our train. I involuntarily quoted the beginning of what is perhaps the loneliest poem ever written: "The crows call and fly quickly to the city, soon it will snow, happy is he who has a home –." "That gives us something in common, dearest," interrupted the delighted lady, deeply moved, "I was Friedrich Nietzsche's friend when we were small. We were both eleven years old, his sister Elizabeth was a few years older; but all three of us played harmoniously together and," she said with emphasis, "the young Friedrich was the father of my little Johanna." Was she still alive, I asked in surprise, did she write poetry, did she resemble Friedrich Nietzsche? The wife of the retired counselor only shook her head in response. But then she told me with eyes alight how one evening her parents' house caught on fire. However, she and her parents and her older sisters and brothers, the maid, the rooster and the hens, even the eggs that were still in the nest were saved. In view of half the inhabitants of Weimar, who had gathered in their doctor's garden to watch the blaze: "And the young Friedrich Nietzsche came racing over with his sister Elizabeth, and we children helped the firemen with the hoses and secretly had a go at the pump and were soaked to the skin. Suddenly the young Friedrich Nietzsche cried: 'Where is Johanna?' White as chalk, he pushed us playmates aside. 'Johanna! Johanna! Johanna is burning to death!' None of the firemen was able to hold back the brave boy. Utterly fearless in the face of death, he ran over the burning steps of the stairs: 'Johanna is burning!' and once again we heard 'Johanna is burning to death!' and we shook with fear. Suddenly we saw him behind the window in the third story – Elizabeth and I clung to each other in distress. Now he had reached my little room, it was spitting fire and thick smoke out into the street. All this took place during a storm, and that was certainly what controlled the fire and kept it from the young Friedrich's body. That is how the inhabitants of Weimar explained it and accounted for the fact that the young Friedrich Nietzsche survived his heroic deed. He, however, brought Johanna alive into my arms, only her flaxen braids were charred, the braids of our beloved Johanna, our beloved doll."

*Dedicated to the admirable, splendid Chancellor
of the Republic Heinrich Brüning*

KARL SONNENSCHEIN

To the great poet and apostle of the poor

Somehow I can't quite
conceive of God as a schoolmaster.
PETER HILLE

I simply say respectfully: Karl Sonnenschein. No decoration can elevate his name. Even his possible canonization will only serve as fair expression to the world that wants to hear and see. He was indeed holy. His soul a devout tricolor flag; its white linen a symbol of his immaculate way, the red stripe kept him alive and alert for his self-sacrificing service to mankind; but the delicate blue led him unimpeded into the higher world. Dr. Karl Sonnenschein and I came from the same city, and when we spoke with each other, the dear old Wupper still flowed, as clear as from its source, through our short, cheerful conversations. Only sometimes a Wuppertal hill rose up, a sharp difference of opinion, a religious one: "She doesn't like Paul!" I could have contradicted him, but his merry indignation suited him so well, indeed, it refreshed him. Because he was glowingly kind. And equally hospitable to all people. Everyone who knocked became the guest of his fine heart, he opened its beating gates to everyone. Never forgot any matter that was told him in confidence. Into his small, modest conference room on George Street came countless people every day, with requests for themselves and for others. It was he, the generous priest, who freed the imprisoned, who didn't leave a stone unturned when it came to helping those who had fought for the poorest of the state and were paying for it: martyrs behind bars. Whether they were Christian or Jewish monks who for the benefit of thousands upon thousands took a stand against the powerful and affluent. And yet they actually wore innocence and guilt, which seen from his broad perspective were *both* martyrs' habits; they just shouldn't fit too tightly. For the same reason that Jesus of Nazareth said: "But I shall spew forth the lukewarm!" Or as it says in our holy Zohar, the first book of the cabala (paraphrased): "The reins of evil should not be brittle, arbitrary reins." Which means that if evil is kept under control nothing bad happens. That is why Karl Sonnenschein wrapped no cloak of exception around anyone – least of all around himself, and he in fact was born to guide us toward good. A religious driver of men, he usually hitched himself before the cart, working himself to death. – It was reassuring when we were of one opinion. We unfortunately seldom had the opportunity for a longer conversation. Soon the short secretary would knock, announcing that another visitor, male or female, had arrived. But when the religious doctor and I met at public events, we were always secretly united by the eternal nature of poets. Karl Sonnenschein was one of the very great poets. Heavenly flowers shone forth from his poetic lectures, and his sermons were like a breath of sweet, fresh air. Yes, dew hung from each of his words. The consecratory psalm for the Catholic reading room that he founded should have been preserved in silver letters. I'm speaking of a Catholic reading room that is open to everyone, otherwise it would not have been brought about by Karl Sonnenschein. He used to ironize praise. Out of modesty, I think; also, the rascal who used to look out of the corner of his eye didn't like it. That's why I once dared to bother him with the story of a love affair in which not I, but my youngest, beautiful girlfriend was involved. She went on at length, forgetting that I had told her the doctor's time was precious. He interrupted her with a smile: "I get it – it's about your fiancé, whose mother refuses to give a Protestant daughter-in-law her blessing. Is that it, my dear child?" "She is even threatening that he will go to purgatory if he marries me, and what is worst of all, she (his mother) would go to purgatory as well, and she would not survive that. And finally, she forced him to break off our relationship." "And did he?" "Yes!" Doctor Sonnenschein (very indignantly): "What a sissy!" But he advised my friend not to throw in the towel. He would very soon be in that neighborhood. Indeed, it seemed to him that he had taught F. when he worked in southern Germany, and he would read him the riot act. He then dictated to his kind secretary a letter to F.'s mother, making it clear to her that if she persisted in trying to separate two lovers, the devils would be justified in doing everything possible to fan the flames of purgatory for her soul. Thanks to Karl Sonnenschein's strong intervention, this amusing little one-act play had a happy ending, and I think it brought fresh air and happiness into his small apartment, where all sadness laid aside its gray clothing. As with all saints, this incident of the heart, coming as it did out of the blue, did him good. All of us, my friends male and female, whether Jews or Christians, secretly called him the Bishop of Berlin. He never found out that we used this term of honor for him. It crossed our lips inadvertently and sounded loving and thankful. I am sorry that he never got to know personally our poet-prophet Peter Hille. Both of them came from Rhineland-Westfalia. But Karl Sonnenschein was involved in writing a great work about Saint Peter Hille. He was working in Lugano, where I had to send him all the Petron books, even my small but blue *Peter Hille Book* that celebrates him, Peter Hille, in legends. Likewise, I had to send him the letters that Peter Hille had once written me, placed together in sequence in a book. These two great people would have celebrated being poets in a way without equal. In Karl Sonnenschein's last years, he occupied himself in particular with Peter Hille. That proves that both were poets. In short, neither of them was bourgeois. They were not stern, but serious, not jovial, but cheerful. When I told him about Peter Hille, he pointed again and again to the young, deep, ascetic face in the frame behind him on the wall —"Did he look like that?" — It was a stigmatized monk that only his friend and he knew about. Once Karl Sonnenschein asked me in all seriousness if Christianity appealed to me at all? "But don't think," he added, "that I intend to convert you. I am far too convinced of your loyalty to your own ancient people." I said to him: "I love and admire the original Christianity, which the bleeding image of the Jew born of God wore on his temple. And I love and admire the apostles, the disciples, and the first followers, who were persecuted and did not persecute! Today, however, I sympathize only with individual people, no matter what their religion. Culture, like the wilderness, heals differences of religious opinion. By the way, I love all people not honored in their native land, as happens to all of us poets – one doesn't even need to be a prophet." Those were actually the last words of our last conversation, and I am honored by the great religious doctor's wish on his last postcard, that I might come to Lugano. He would so dearly have liked to hear from me about Peter Hille – like flowers picked from the heart. That makes me proud, and I thank Karl Sonnenschein in spirit for his invitation.

There was a long, long drawn-out funeral procession along all the gray streets, past all the crumbling, black old houses. The dwellings situated at the rear of these houses had been visited almost daily by "the good man who died," said the poorest people in the row beside me with a sigh. "Yes, we all know, he did only good in his life, we all knew that." It sounds cold to speak of an irrecoverable loss, because even if Karl Sonnenschein can no longer be active among us, he nevertheless lives on with undiminished value in our memory. I think we all walked for hours behind the hearse that brought him to divine rest. Countless people escorted him, little orphan children and great, lonely, rich and poor people who loved him. We felt ourselves incredibly drawn along, and walked as if under a moon in broad daylight. Before I threw my white lilacs into his still open grave, with our Hebrew prayer as old as God on my lips, I saw God the Father gaze down amazed from heaven, since the people who have been released from his earth, the blond or black-haired, light- or dark-skinned, do not lie beside each other in one graveyard, no matter what

they believed on earth – but here he saw them all under one
sky. Melting snow wept over our mourning faces.

> An angel walks invisibly through our city
> To gather love for the one who has gone home,
> Who loved his neighbor – more than – himself. –

> A tear for the loved one,
> An eye that shines for his soul
> A pure word from the red leaf of your mouth –

> For him, to whom you confessed all your worries;
> His bittersweet comfort already contained his deed.

RENATE AND THE ARCHANGEL GABRIEL

Through the summer nights, Renate danced on the high wire
over all the houses and church steeples of the city. But when it
turned cold, the little girl sold wax matches in cute little boxes;
each one had a picture painted on it: Undine, or a ship, or two
cherubs that actually looked like Max and Moritz, even if they
did have two wings on their shoulders. And for the past year
Renate had to take her two-year-old brother (who could
hardly say "Nate") along with her in the uneasy semidarkness
of the bustling streets. But her thin arm tenderly embraced the
little boy, who was wrapped in a colorfully flowered cloth.
Renate had big blue eyes and long black lashes and her hair
cut short like a boy's, not because that happened to be in style
at the time. Long hair had caused her mother's death, which
she could not get over. She, too, had been a tightrope-walker,
and just a few years previously, Miss Rosa still hovered over
the tightened ropes, her sparkling toy on her strong shoulders,
and was gently carried through the whispering air. Until the
famous Miss also wanted to take on the unbridled whirlwind.

It tousled her long dark curls and ultimately blocked her view with the black silk, so that the poor mother lost her balance, fell out of the clouds down to earth, and was dead on the spot. Her little Renate, however, sat up there like a little bird on one of the thick wooden handles of the scaffolding and waited unsuspectingly until someone brought her down to see her dead mother. . . .

Since the death of her daring mother, she became a little afraid of the walk with the moon, and she had a fever again and again after that night of pain. And the little tightrope-walker felt that doing business on the firm ground of the paved streets was nevertheless a privilege. Frequently the flushed child experienced hypnogogic images, from which she seemed to recover, but she was not spared terrible fever dreams, in which she saw how her little Edmund turned into a ladybug on her neck, crawled over her striped dress, crawled laboriously over the hill of her knee and down her trembling legs. Arriving at the world, he began to fly, and before her eyes, wide with fear, and her paralyzed hands, he disappeared into the departing day. And Renate searched and searched for him, shuddering with each ticktack of the many unmindful steps that hurried by, any of which could have crushed her sweet little brother. She cried, and over her slight limbs and her back fire-goblins and snowmen danced the polonaise and shook her body, and the least of her losses came only as quietly as a cloud into her consciousness, she had let fall the basket with her wares. Renate's misery became extreme. If only her little Edmund had at least flown into a garden and had lit on a soft leaf, that would be some consolation for her, but Edmund was certainly already dead and lay somewhere on the roadway with his little feet torn off and his tiny red body crushed; where would she find it in the pale shine of the light. "Dear Edmund, come back! Dear little Edmund, do come back!" called Renate pleadingly into the evening, and sympathetic people put pieces of money into her hot hand and listened in astonishment as the poor girl told them her little brother had drowned in a murky puddle, or a street-boy had seen his black eyes glowing on his back, had taken him with him and put him in a cigar box, just as her friends also did. O God, how frightened her little brother would be in the dungeon! . . . The glassy advertising columns at the edge of the streets and in the squares chatted on undisturbed about the colorful pleasures of the city; and the colors playing on the sidewalk from the neon lights gave tormenting interpretations to Renate's imaginings. She was resting in front of a movie theater. The last show began at nine. Her blue eyes were fixed on, indeed glued to one of the posters that showed a troupe of itinerant entertainers. She herself was also painted on the big arc, the triumphant queen of the sky. With a glowing sphere in her hand, she stood there over the cathedral on the tightrope under all the stars and gave a friendly wave to the spectators. "Please, dear young lady, let me in!" Renate begged the cashier and shyly put only her poor harried little heart into her outstretched hand. That was noticed by the great archangel Gabriel, who paid for the fevered child and went in with her. The show had already begun. Just then the little Renate was dancing on the tightrope, and the crowd gazed at her in wonder and applauded with thousands of hands. The Archangel Gabriel knew the little Renate. It was he who had taken her from the arms of her falling mother and set her down under the sky. He said to her: "Now you can look down on the entire city from up high, and somewhere you will find your little brother again." The Angel Gabriel was not a phantasm of little Renate's. He was really sitting there in the front row between the people, beside the searching child, in his long, sky-blue robe. I myself sat in the audience and stared at him in wonder. As soon as a street tried to hide from Renate's gaze, the Archangel Gabriel dragged it back again by the chimney of its tallest house, so that the dear girl could look at it in the light. And finally Renate discovered a sparkling drop of blood sitting on a meadow flower that was still alive in the suburbs. She carefully pushed her little Edmund, while looking around fearfully in the movie theater, as a thief a gem, over her fingertip into her trembling hand, and she hid her hand under the warm, flowered cloth, under which he had been slumbering uninterruptedly. Suddenly, the basket with the matches was also hanging on Renate's arm again. She looked up questioningly at her very tall neighbor, the Archangel Gabriel, who began to take great delight in the dear little matchboxes. And he bought a box with a picture of a ship on it from the dear girl for his dear God at home in heaven. Then he recognized the two rogues of angels on another box and he told the child that they were the two who were always trampling with their feet on the thunder drum and scratching with their fingernails across the brightly polished lightning, annoying the fixed stars, powdering the moon with twilight dust and eating the golden Mama's honey. And Renate looked again over all the buildings of the city, sitting in the audience beside the magnificent – "I tell you" – archangel Gabriel, who looked after her and her little brother on earth and in the heights. Amen . . .

THE CHILD AMONG THE MONTHS

His grandchild is already alive, and the songbirds are singing in the forest. When I looked into the garden courtyard two months ago, everything was full of leaves and happy. The little acacia wore a green head of curls, the mountain ash dreamed of her jewelry of corals, and the tallest tree waved coquettishly in its new Valenciennes; that made the broad, powerful oak tree laugh, really! The entire garden courtyard heard it, every stirring blade of grass, and I am its witness. I love to talk about trees, their boughs really carry the most splendid toys – and no one can get me out of the forest too easily! Finally, the child of the months is on the calendar. Now the world storms ahead into the sun: "All the birds are already here, all the birds, all!" . . . Finally he came, the first of May, the Messiah of the months. A gentle heart holds the word: May. A promising, flattering word, letters that accompany one richly into the summer. The sky knows that and is in a blissful blue mood. I am no longer able to change as quickly as he can from gray to sky-colors, from dull to bright; I mean: to conjure up laughter from tears. All of us froze too long to simply abandon ourselves to the newly arrived sunbeams, to sparkle like playing children who want for nothing and have all, out of whom the Buddha probably created nirvana. I heard the smallest of them already chirping early in the morning, but the cock was also crowing in between, even if more foggily than usual; he is supposed to have been served up roasted on some table at noon, and it is his spirit that keeps the remaining hens in check. To think that I also devour animals, and like to eat meat best of all, is something for which I have not been able to forgive myself to this very day! We people even crave refined, rotten animal dishes and are not content, as animals are, to take the animal fresh from nature and enjoy the taste of it. First of all we pluck the shimmering feathers from the small, slaughtered dove, rip the entrails out of the still-warm body, the heart, the heart! – Put the robbed little bird, the head-nodding, friendly, unsuspecting little animal in the frying pan and braise it. "Please, don't interrupt me," I know, the cannibals are almost as cruel as we are, but they at least dance a pious – if greasy – dance of joy around their victim, and light a high fire around their delicious white human dish until it gets a crust on it. It is by no means my intent to defend man-eaters, but I would nevertheless like to mention that some of the tribes that enjoy human meat subscribe to the superstition that when they eat white-man cutlet they are also devouring his intelligence. May the great idol of the cannibals keep their excuses healthy. Yes, it seems we constantly need antidotes. Meat needs meat. Fruits seem like something dead to us, prob-ably because the apple once brought death into the world. We shouldn't let ourselves get unnerved; fruit, just like humans and animals, is made of living flesh and blood, like everything else that is alive in the world. And even the seductive apple, the pear, the peach, the apricot, the cherry, the orange, the fig, the date, the triplet sisters: raspberries, strawberries, blackber-ries; lastly the banana, and in addition the many vegetables: white and red cabbage, brussels sprouts, carrots, asparagus and its noble brides, the green bean and the wax bean; I almost forgot spinach, savoy cabbage, peas and lentils (with roasted bread cubes), cucumbers and radishes, horseradish, and other kinds of vegetables should really be adequate along with po-tatoes for our meal. Please don't read between the lines of my vegetarian notes and suspect me of having a vegetable stand at the market; my story, which ends well in its conception, is by no means meant to serve as advertising. Everything, every-thing is alive in the world, and this first of May brings me new proof of that again. I so love the world and regret that the international freedom of movement always just floats past me. It costs money. My fellow man fears that if he gives me some money I will no longer be creative – especially since he spends his days reading my works. I am a bird, blown out of the colorful air. Anyone who has not yet experienced the ef-fect of fresh air should convince himself of its berry, and should meet me sometime in the morning when I am intoxicated by the gold foaming grape of heaven. I fly with greater stamina than the migratory bird, the wings alone are not enough; it's the breath, the breath set in motion, the wing-beat of the blood, the dissolution of the brain, the devotion to God. People shouldn't always want to think something! Breath is strength! And it is the original sin not to breathe. It is a "virtue," though, to play a role in living, that is, to breathe in measured breaths. The fakirs breathe no other way. One in a tall turban once said to me that I had been a seagull at the time of the Ice Age; that is why I am awakened some nights by my own scream. One should respect that, basically. My neighbor in the next room, though, has complained, and my life is endangered. What we do not understand, we despise and like to kill. Anyone who has never heard the helpless tree cry out when it is being cut and has not seen it bleed, or who has not seen the veins of the rock smoulder when dynamite is pushed into the crevice of its stone, should spend more time studying the story of Creation. I will never forget you, young, trembling, white calf, as you were dragged to the slaughterhouse. No angel averted the hand of the apprentice with knife held high.

Where Is the One Who Is Most Alive?

Who ever felt his pulse in the stone of the past! "God created the earth by pulling himself together to make room for it." The venerable Rabbi Lurja, the cabalist, taught me this celestial wisdom. So the Godhead made room for the universe, bestowed upon it its atmosphere, from which everything grew and thrived, even the temperatures, the characteristics of the countries. To preserve the order of the world is mankind's only mission. To breathe: the original law that keeps creation in motion. From this God-thesis separated out the words: "Thou shalt not kill!" When fear hindered people and caused their breath to stop, death arose. Death means dissolution, and dissolution means, basically, in God's terms: losing time, and we should make every effort to keep ourselves alive as long as possible and likewise not kill our fellow man under the influence of some hostile feeling. But conserve ourselves for the all-breath power of the work of creation and its all-aliveness. And since everything from human beings to pebbles is a creation, and breathes, we should proceed more conscientiously. Even before God, or especially before God, it is not seemly to hold one's breath, because to fear God does not mean to be afraid of God but to revere him by breathing devoutly within the infinite organism, breathing in and out with the eternal wings of breath. – How gold melts the dying eye, nothing lives more intensely in the world than these two shining metals. The narrowest chain of gold flows around your neck, an island of thousands of living drops. If one thinks about it logically, there is no death, only a pause of the mind, a grave that we dig through no fault of our own by holding our breath. The result is dissolution!

Where Does God Revolve?

He whispers warnings around our heart, previously he surged around his peoples. Does he lean against the space that he cast off from himself and called the universe, or does it support itself on him? What is God's physical relationship to the world, given that he shaped himself? Facing backwards or sideways? Presumably face-on. Are we now disconnected from God, or are we watered from his original vein? This would bear out the workings of the soil. Therefore, I explain God's omnipotence to the world like that of the mother to the child. He separated the water from the land, let heaven ascend, and found everything to be good. How should I, a dreaming person, understand that his image is made of inferior material and the soul of his image suffers damage, crashes into things, and loses its way in bewilderment and discontent. We are simply here to work on the original colossus of the world, to uphold its laws, to keep the universe alive, to breathe uninterruptedly. Only when we noble egoists serve the cosmos do *we remain alive*. Whoever kills himself or his fellow man out of passion or meanness robs something from the power of breath that keeps our Father's creation in motion. My deep breath unites me with the universe. How I welcome, therefore, the first of May, the golden child of the months, with its warm breath! Oh, I love the warmed air and breathe it in and out in an eternal breath, drink it from the jug of the clouds, from the cup of the stars, from God's host table. And the winds that come over the rivers water me and I steal strength from the storms that blow from ocean to ocean.

MY SILENT PRAYER

We close our eyes in the evening without fear; accustomed to the brief, temporary death from the day we are born. Some people pray before they go to sleep, seldom a one of them with the thought of never waking again. If the actual sleep of death concluded a person's life often or even occasionally, then a person in the sleep of death would have no more fear of temporary death than of the sleep that interrupts life! And would regard death as a companion who finds the way home again to the waking state. Death, however, is final and inexorable. One cannot come back over its "forbidden" path, because it is no green path or paved street, it is the forbidden *spiritual* way that leads into suspended nothingness. Morning light awakens the sleeping soul in the warm body and gives to the quick new excitement. But who awakens the person who has died and gives him or her the incomparable gift of eternal life, the secret prize of redemption? Every creature, every thing on earth works all the time – there is no lazing about – in order to stay alive, since to breathe is the purest form of original work, indeed the original virtue of the world. Everything that exists adheres to the oscillating breath of creation. And the final death would be an irrecoverable loss for the heart-works of the original organism if being born and dying did not go hand in hand and mean only a change of state. Breath is divinity that has passed by, that we breathe in and out to keep the world alive and give it motion. Activities other than *breathing* are basically superfluous to God. Totally convinced of this truth, the Indian priest abandons himself to spiritual drink. He who has been released from life rests in the Godhead, *in the breath,* and the survivor experiences his dear departed one as much more merged with himself and in a greater variety of ways, because he is breathing him in and out and constantly experiencing the resting soul released from this life. I have always endeavored to dig, not for gold but for God; sometimes I have touched heaven. I have dug for the eternal one, not out of audacious arrogance, but out of a religious desire for adventure. That is why I sneaked away from suffocating boudoirs and studios, between whose walls one often brought God down off the wall, framed in metaphysics, for discussion, just as one would treat one of the paintings by the hand of the hospitable artist. For years, I spent the evenings by myself reading in the books that are printed in the hereafter. Not as one usually reads line by line, but walking on paths with the people from the ancient stories who laid the roots for humanity. Whoever takes in the material of the Testaments *in that manner* has eaten of the bread of life. The person of the Bible is not able to give more to his grandchild than to pass on to him the light in the word. And when my unforgettable dear boy said to me: "Tomorrow or the day after tomorrow I will die, . . ." after a while asserting sincerely: " . . . You are strong, that I always knew, but that you are so strong as to keep death away from me for months, for that I am grateful to you . . ." – I thought, even though deeply embarrassed by the praise from my heroically suffering child, I thought of the sacred manna that I have eaten. In the last weeks of his life, my boy became absorbed in the falling of the leaves, and he often quietly accompanied the setting sun, whose gold seemed to him the most precious in the world. A mighty tree stood in front of the window. Its leaves formed a domed canopy in the summer. "Ten-family tree," I sometimes joked. The birds came, and flew away again to look for worms for their young birds. One time they all remained entranced on the boughs. A number of summer children dressed in blue went singing past the listening tree, and the older birds informed the young ones that a piece of heaven had fallen to earth. Often, in the evening, many, many little eyes looked through our window directly at the electric moon, which they held to be a special star that thrived between the warm walls of our hothouse. When October came, we seldom saw them sitting on the branches anymore; the crumbs that we put out for them remained untouched and hardened overnight. My poor beautiful boy compared his emaciated limbs to the bare branches – in the darkness I held the sorrowful look in his eyes before me through the night. On the evening before he died, he seemed to me like a two-year-old again. I could have carried him and sung him into the sleep of death, his tall body had become so light. I thought so much about God, and now he was picking the most beautiful star from the festival of my heart. I called to him in expectation of an answer; after all, he spoke to the first people, to the patriarchs, but they still had perfect hearing. When a child dies, one knows that space and time is a condition, and one has only to kneel to reach one's child in death. It is the sky, the blue transfiguration, that separates the dying one from the one who is left behind. We living people are dark, so dark that we never find ourselves. It is written in the cabala that the Godhead stripped off its darkness before creating the world. It is to be understood in no other way than that God once had a body of his own just as we do, that he redeemed himself, which is what we call dying, and, freed from the shell, let his light shine through the primal chaos. It is so easy to maintain there is no God. And the logic goes only far enough with most people to be able to prove that they are hungry and should buy a bite to eat. We who are hungry are able neither to buy nor to pick fruit from the tree. But we stand in bright expectation, set with stars. Thus, in the beginning was actually not the word but the deed: God transfigured himself from a visible to an invisible God. That is to say: he abandoned the prison of the body, and maintains the universe spiritually. Only in this way am I able to comprehend the human form, which God created in his own original image. And I ask myself why one should despise this original image, the flesh, the mortal frame for the soul, especially since we do take pleasure in the luxuriantly crowded leaves of the forest and of every individual tree, so why not in the beauty of the bodily temple, which preserves in itself a treasure, the holiest of all things, the soul. I rely on God, because how often have I put my grief and my joy in his hand, and now my child, my grief and my joy. One says nothing into the wind that is not carried further into invisibility. Summer turns into fall, winter into spring, and death into life, and the youngest life into death. There must be a God, given the cyclical nature of world order, but there would still be a God even if the stars walked on earth and the trees grew on the sky. And yet we experience everything blindly through milky wisdom, the wisdom of the world. We can't forcibly leap over levels of insight, but we should want to discover God, to dig for him, until we discover him.

THE DAY OF ATONEMENT

There is no Jew who does not think of his parents on this day, the holiest day of the year. For father and mother, the Day of Atonement was the birthday of Jewishness. And so it is for all Jews in all countries and continents and for their children and children's children, and children's children's children. The need for atonement cannot be eradicated from the world of the Jew, who must someday stand before God as his creation in his own image. The weary, obstinate children of God set aside enmity on this day and smile in harmony. Even on the eve of the Day of Atonement we only tiptoed around so as not to scare away the sweet devotion. On one's damask one sets the table for the great angel of atonement who is born anew every year in every Jewish household. And for the daughter and the son who are far away from their parents' house, the Day of Atonement acts as a reminder, a memory that has taken shape. The star of peace shines from their foreheads. In a white robe, Jew carries the Day of Atonement gently to Jew, and also makes friends anew with other people of the city. All rancor melts in his heart; "quarrels," it turned out, arose in error. Our hands are here today to place themselves in yours. Poisonous plants grow on the site of the confrontation that remains unresolved. I think of home; the candles were already lit in the twilight of the previous evening, only my father was still missing from the peaceful table that was decorated with flowers. Its flower beds were not at all disturbed by the transparent, milky-white porcelain, or by the steaming soup in the tureen. We had been hearing my father's restless steps overhead for some time, though they were lighter than usual. He used to use the entire second story of the house for getting dressed. Now and then, startled curses lulled into a psalm would sound from the hallway as he emerged from the bedroom. But even there he did not succeed in front of the first, second, or even third mirror in pushing the collar-stud into the small opening in his collar. Either the button had grown overnight or the devil was behind it. First of all Dore, "the ginger cat," our cook, hurried to help him, but we soon heard her slinking down the steps miaowing spitefully. She had even quit – temporarily; she sent Elise up to Mr. Schüler, she was more patient and listened to my father when he explained to her the significance of the Day of Atonement. Also, she always pulled out the pair of boots that didn't pinch his feet, selecting them from his regiment of boots, all twelve pairs of which presented themselves bolt upright in a row of shiny leather along the wall. My father loved snazzy boots, and also a well-fitted suit. His snow-white hair and beard washed with violet-scented soap, all spruced up, the ends of his moustache twirled, my father finally expectantly approached the Day of Atonement dinner with eyes averted in a holy expression. We children could hardly suppress our laughter any longer until he himself laughingly reprimanded us because of the solemnity of the occasion. And now we sat around the table, not exactly a family, but a small world unto ourselves, each of us a quite different person of various colors of blood that did mix with each other and for better or for worse separated again; countries united on God's day. I was the youngest and was always allowed to sit beside my adored mama, who secretly put a candy into the pocket of my little plaid dress. Beside her, I felt like the eternal life that had once brought me into the world, and on this evening, in the warm velvet of the atoning room, I remembered how I used to play on the grassy slope under her heart. Oh, when I think back to that, my eyes shut themselves again half blind, and when I write about it, the letters of the alphabet bleed on the snow of the paper. – I was always the first one to get my heated little plate filled, then my father, who loved bone-marrow dumplings, he kept secret count of the number that mercilessly disappeared into the various plates with the soup-ladle. Mind you, he would not have noticed if the bone-marrow dumplings had been kneaded out of cardboard flour. – Next to my father on his left, my sister Martha Theresia was thinking dreamily, with her almond-shaped eyes rolled up in her olive-colored face. My second sister Annamarie, the most beautiful flower in the Wupper Valley, sometimes used to push her arm through the strong hussar's arm of my second brother. There was something so helpless about her delicateness. Between my second brother and my oldest brother, who had traveled home from his academy for the Day of Atonement, my youngest brother, Paul Karl Schüler, sat and ate with great modesty and friendliness. In the year that he was born, my mother was inspired by the age of Schiller, which was in vogue at the time. My brother Paul would still go to school, and to high school. He wrote poetry in Latin and Greek, and he and my dear mother secretly read their poetry to each other in the living room. He helped me with my schoolwork. Those were hours on our own. In nature study, he taught me to be good to the poorest people and to come to the assistance of tormented animals. He told me the names of all the stones in his splendidly sparkling stone collection, and often he took me by the hand and climbed up the hill with me, at the foot of which our house was located. We climbed up into the forest and picked beechnuts and wild berries. He knew all the trees and shrubs and flowers, as if he had created the world with God. "He was certainly present," said my friend Emmy in the schoolyard, "because he is a saint, an Apollo." Just as he was drawn in our world history book, standing leaning against a pillar and looking terribly distinguished, that's how my tall blond youngest brother looked. To my oldest brother, however, I remained a stranger. He was much older than I, and since he was seldom home, I did not succeed in stringing him onto a thread between my parents and me. With the help of my fairy-tale book, I fantasized about the prince who had lost his way, because his being a brother of mine seemed more mysterious to me with each passing year. Until once, on his arrival home, he pulled me out from between porters behind whom I had hidden myself, bewitched by his fascinating nature, and slapped me across the face for my impoliteness, admonishing me like a master: "To remember me by." That was the cause of total estrangement between him and me, between sister and brother, the equally loved children of our parents. Yes, my brothers and sisters were all good-looking, resembling my parents, and I could judge that well, as a small, not-yet-separated offshoot of my mother, who together with me secretly admired her big children. – After the soup came fish in butter sauce and sweet potatoes. Every time my father had to ask to make sure the fish wasn't eel, since Moses had forbidden him to eat it – because it fed on corpses. . . . And then came fillet garnished with vegetables, and mirabelle compote, which we two children, my father and I, ate with a passion. And he at least seemed not to notice that my oldest sister filled his plate with all the rest of the preserved fruits while he continued his lecture: one should stop eating when one still felt hungry; that was the advice given to his parents and twenty-two sisters and brothers and himself by the famous officer of health of his hometown in Westfalia, who had been the physician for a thousand incurably ill patients. Until a flame suddenly shot through the door opened by the serving-girl, the flame encircling the plum pudding. My mother loved to be served this illuminated food for dessert, and I was proud of this exclusive, dangerous dish. Plum pudding with fire and wine sauce! In the end, my father stuck the big table-napkin in his jacket pocket, a habit he could not be broken of even on weekdays, he covered his dear head with his hand, because the head must be covered out of humility before God when one prays; and quickly, as he used to mumble through the end of the Extemporale before the end of school, he mumbled through our most venerable, regal prayer: "Schema jïsroël adonâ elohenu adonâ echod."* Whereupon, on the arm of my oldest sister, his daughter Martha Theresia, he proceeded out of the house through the evening streets into the east end of the city, into the temple of the synagogue. He had long since forgotten my mother's request that he at least behave during the sermon. For my father, the Day of Atonement was the biggest thrill of the year. On this day, he even forgot his buildings and plans. My father was the most exuberant person I have ever met in my life, he always had a rascal sitting somewhere on the upholstery of his red heart. He was certainly not happy because he was deep (as I hear the literary figures asking me) – he was exuberant because he was expansive. He raged and towered, he smashed things up; there was no stemming his mood, and he *could* put his head through the wall. Suffering and worry encountered him in carnival bells, and joy tore his door off its hinges. But his anger – he could thunder powerfully, which occurred against humorous backdrops that threatened to collapse. Often the maids hid me, although my father never used his fists. They hid me in the kitchen cupboard that was set into

*Hear, O Israel, the Lord is our God, the Lord is One.

the wall. The workers had their afternoon naps in there on the ground floor when they were building it. It ended then, in the event that he found me, with my being punished – by not being allowed to go to school. And today, yet again, he slammed the synagogue door thoughtlessly like our poor-house door, after he and my sister had walked into the inside of the holy place, into the castle, and his voice, which had a roguish prank to report to every Jew, could be heard right up to the seats at the back of the balcony, where Martha Theresia used to sit. And when my father had finally discovered his daughter up there in her white feather hat, he again forgot to keep himself under control, if the girls beside her were not to his taste.

So he disrupted the service without intending the sin, be-cause he fasted faithfully, without complaint, without even staying at home in thought, where the water was already boil-ing in the coffeemaker to make the mocha that my father used to drink first of all! The star considerately came out from the clouds a quarter of an hour earlier, as usual in the evenings of the year, but the Christian castellan wasn't late either, who turned to my father: "Mr. Schüler, Ah'm 'fraid Ah'll lose ma jowb here in de Jewish church if Ah don't most obedyently get you outta here." My father took that readily in good spirits; the servant in the synagogue was the brother of his old chum Robert and knew what he was doing. He earned himself a thaler each time if he also fetched my sister from the gallery, leading her by her fingertips and gently bringing her to my father in the little synagogue garden, where the two of them waited for their friends. While my oldest, sixteen-year-old sis-ter was praying for us, I had carried out her order promptly and heard the whistled signal of the pupil in the top form: "If I stand in dark midnight. . . ." Even if he was disappointed to see the little sister instead of his flame, he did hand over to me, stroking my bobbed hair, the essay that he used to write every month for his adored Martha Theresia. His likeness lay between the cover and the page. I thought myself endlessly important as go-between, although I sometimes got the signals confused, because in one of the houses that bordered on our little street (Schülers' Lane), there was yet another admirer, the admirer of my second sister, with the long chestnut-brown hair. Walter's heart used to waft out of his restless breast by six o'clock, and he would sing: "I saw your picture in a dream. . . ." The Star of David under the brow of the cupola of the sacred palace of God sent out its rays when the Jews were leaving the temple, and still today I believe in its reach, because I see it with wide-awake, open eyes. With pure devotion, bent over the Torah in front of the altar, the cantor, the holy man sings the psalms of atonement as old as the stars. It's nice to be a Jew, if one has never avoided that in order to reach a goal more quickly, if one has remained true to that and grown closer to it, not seduced by any external vanity, but washed by the River Jordan. Who can tear me away from the ancient bones of Jehovah, the unshakable rock! The Jew passes tests daily, humiliation tastes bitter to his palate, but strengths do arise out of it, although not every Jew is successful in keeping the original fragrance in his blood. The Messiah has already walked on earth. Neither the Jews nor any other peoples were ready to value and to preserve in its authenticity this gift from heaven, "he came not to destroy the law, but to fulfill the law." He measured the pulse of his people, he dispelled sadness and condemned halfheartedness, but he also attempted to settle arguments. He will come again at the end of the world, the Day of Atonement incarnate, the Messiah. Because only the reconciliation of all people is able to uplift and deliver us. A chair at the table remains free for the Messiah, as a child I hid my best toy between the back and the seat for him. He would

133

find it. The fasting of the stomach is not enough if the soul is not stripped of all trumpery so that it gleams: "Make room for God." What counts is the fasting of the soul, because in these great hours it should fill itself with inexhaustible, joyful love of the Day of Atonement.

MY BOY

But I am making an effort to write truthfully about him. There is no denying that it is difficult and rare to make a statement about one's own child, especially when he was so modest and unsophisticated a child. Any attempt to put him in the limelight went against his grain. My son was beautiful. I am not saying anything new or unknown with this truth. He was so beautiful that I often made the effort, even when he was a child – my little Paul – to buy him suits or hats that subdued his beauty. I did that out of caution or out of fear that he could be stolen from me someday. My son was a dear boy; the most heartfelt and therefore most meaningful thing that one can say of one's child. That would have been enough for me, but he was also one of the most talented people I have known. His playfulness combined charmingly with his talent. He loved to play the harmonica. Whenever I praised him, he begged me not to make anything special of it when talking to other people. He said everyone could do it! Nevertheless, I always had to buy him a new harmonica for his birthday – he played it with his tongue! And I was supposed to take Lothar Homeyer along with me to help choose it, since he was not only a good painter but also knew music. Later on, my boy had a clock collection; he would scrutinize the working of the little wheels for hours, as the machinist watches his machines in operation. He was precise, and that stood him in good stead with his drawings. As a little boy, he liked to climb on the scaffolding of houses that were being built. When I was looking for him on our Catherine Street in Halensee, he suddenly called to me out of the blue between the beams and the air. I kept many of the little drawings he did before he was two years old, which were not to be compared with the usual talented drawings of youthful artists. When he was one year old, he would insist that his governess put him on his feet whenever they went by new buildings. Then he collected little pieces of lime. He also used to pick up electric coals in front of the street lamps on the sidewalk. Then his little white pants would be pitch-black. How often his good governess, Mrs. Müller, would scold me for scribbling again on the floor of Paul's room, which she had scrubbed! The little houses and trees were really nice, she said, but that just wouldn't do! I got suspicious. And we caught him in the act of using his little hands to pull a chair closer to the edge of the bed, then carefully climbing out of bed and decorating the floor with a piece of the chalk that he had loaded into the wagons of his train. Needless to say, the elderly Mrs. Müller and I were really shocked. As we were when my boy, still in his high chair, drew a crow and said "I've drawn a crow that steals meat." Best of all, he liked to draw animals, and his progress was extraordinary. When I sometimes took him along on Sunday afternoons to the "Café of the West," he would sit down all by himself at a marble table behind the stairs. No one was allowed to see what he was drawing. Not even Elsa, his playmate. I don't think I'm being indiscreet if I divulge what my boy confided in me one evening when I had taken his shoes and socks off and put him to bed and he was noticeably lost in thought. In answer to my concerned questioning as to what was wrong, his melancholy answer was: "I'm thinking about Elsa. She always plays with my watch-chain, and I pull at her curls. When I am seventeen years old, I will visit her and ask her: 'Elsa, do you want to be my wife?'" Otherwise, he was bubbling over as a little boy, and always came leaping through the door: "Mother, now I want to go to the stars – and see the points on them." His favorite word was *Persia*. Every evening I beat up an egg for him with sugar. Once we got home somewhat later than usual. For the first time, sitting on his governess' arm, he had seen the glowing sunset. When I then went to prepare his egg again, he called: "Mother, mother, don't bweak the sun." I can't refrain from telling about a few very personal events, I simply must! On account of the great warmth that moves me. When my boy was fourteen years old, I showed his drawings to the man who was then President of the Academy of the Arts, Professor Manzel. He feared that I was telling him a fib out of maternal vanity, because it was impossible, he said, for a fourteen-year-old to draw with such skill. But he was convinced. Because one day my Paul came with me. The professor sent him first of all for a year to the master studio of his old friend and teacher in Munich; although he would have liked to teach him himself from the start. Karl Arnold, the great Simplizissimus artist, once said about my boy's drawing: "He doesn't draw, he swims across the paper." A talent such as my boy had should not be allowed to become rigid in the factory of the studio. It was a long time before he started drawing again on his own initiative and could "swim." He had inherited his talent from his forefathers.

I am sorry and pained that my boy was so often away from home. I lamented to him: "If only I were a simple middle-class mother with a house and a hearth!" Then he answered each time with the same two words: "Better not!" He knew how I was always worrying about him. I was not only his mother and he my son, he was my little brother. We were brothers – and my pain was double. Like me, he was searching for –

136

happiness. The miracle of love. A charming Don Juan, who is always just looking for the special one! "Dear Mother," he asked me, "wait a minute here at the store window." He had seen a girl with eyes the blue of cornflowers. He loved corn-flower-blue eyes, and hair as blond as wheat. He loved the Nordic type – although he was once interested in a girl from Manila. He was charmed by the Swedish films. When we had an argument, one thing was certain: we would be sitting beside each other expectantly that evening at the movies.

Thousands and thousands of drawings and exercises from my incredibly diligent son lie organized in trunks. In his later years, he would practice the same nose and same mouth or the same expression of the eyes again and again. It was not enough for him simply to have the drawings that he had picked from his young heart lying around. He stared in wonder at the painters Rembrandt and Franz Marc. Sometimes, as a little boy, he drew things for me that were so funny that the tears ran down my cheeks. He was the comedian on paper. Nobody even suspected that he was actually a first-class actor. Judging by his great beauty and elegance, he would have been given romantic roles to play. An artist visited us in Davos, and my Paul attempted to liven up her stay by masterfully imitating schoolmasters or professors of the old style lying deathly ill in bed. She doubled up with laughter. He admired George Grosz immensely, as a person and as an artist. Gottfried Benn was his poet. Otherwise, good verses filled him with envy. No one but I had the right to write poetry. He was, indeed, outstandingly jealous. That came from his bit of Spanish blood. It filled him with sadness if he suspected that I was interested in others. Sometimes he would not let me have any peace until I bought myself a dress or a pair of shoes. It wasn't right that a poetess should go around looking like I did. I knew then, every time, that he also wanted something, but first I was supposed to get something for myself. In the foyer of a hotel in Zürich we met Frank Wedekind with his wondrously beautiful Tilly. He was so surprised by my boy's beauty and by the simplicity of his artistic nature that I asked him not to talk about it anymore in front of Paul. My boy resembled my two flowery sisters, above all my dear mother. There was a rose in the dimple on his chin, and his hair shone darkly. He was a grand seigneur. How he would kiss a lady's hand! His courtly manner was like a comical caricature. And he knew how to play with children! We often went into the vicinity of a little orphanage to bring the children candy. Nobody knows how nice he was to the poor children. He rolled around on the ground with them. Drew series of pictures for them. Only when we got home were incredible tragedies portrayed in drawings. He absolutely detested vanity. He was always as if he had just turned twelve, but was as serious as a full-grown person; to be sure, he often relegated his seriousness to the pocket of his fur vest. His bubbling exuberance had bouquet.

One year before the death of my boy, I had a vision. King David sat in my room – it was late in the evening, he wore a black robe and a black turban. His eyes were like ashes. He remained a long time, sitting beside me. Yes, terrible events are always preceded by terrible overtures. – And so ends the story of my dear boy.

THE SUN

When I ride back to Berlin from my lecture tours, I look out the train window, and my eyes leaf through the living picture-book of the world, and on my last trip home, it happened that the setting sun actually spoke with me. I was crying a little and invited its sympathy, but I was like a child, with a tear still hanging from its lashes. It was seen by the white sun, which I at first thought was the moon; it was already past twilight, and I was tired and sleepy from looking at the striped fields and the meadows' delight in flowers, and the trees marching along; the fir trees and poplars run with giant strides out of the way of the rushing train. I think they hate the sprinter, it frightens the birch brides and the harmony of growth, its breath makes the silver grasses in the fields dusty and their heavenly ally is happy to rain on the flag of gray and black sparks that blows from the train. I gazed into the pale white moon, into the little tent of peace. "It's the sun," said a fellow passenger. She understood the geography of heaven and earth better than I, because even before the train stopped, she knew where we would stop; she was familiar with even the smallest village. However, I asked the faithful, white filled circle again: "Are you the sun? So light up my belief in this world in which I have to live, year after year, hour after hour with its sixty minutes; have to stay awake, subject of the most everyday chamberlain. And I would like to sleep a thousand times, if that were possible in a miracle minute." A frightened rabbit ran across the path, and for the first time I saw a deer in its natural habitat, with yellowy-brown branches on his head. He wasn't frightened either by the tempestuous insistence of my heart or by the speed of our machine, and I smiled questioningly at the white sun, which suddenly, in response to a magic word from God, turned into a glowing red ball and – fell into my lap.

THE SEA

Once upon a time the sea, too, was enveloped by a body, before it roared away. The sea is the far-streaming "remaining" soul of the world. The sea is of this world. But the spirit of God hovers over its water. We dive into the sacred element and are released from all of earth's gravity. Ships glide over the ocean from continent to continent. One would like always to embrace those blissfully roaring waters in worship. It is a release without equal to surrender oneself to the waves; the creature celebrates its union with the sea. I look admiringly over the rushing table, decorated ceremoniously with pearls. – Now it is night, but the eternal water has a silvery shine like my liberated heart. I spread my wings out wide and know nothing more than: to hover – to be a bird! Below me a wave breaks, a sullen nightingale sings its exciting song. Armies of white-belted water storm to the beach, making me an island. I have discovered myself!! Who is here with me? Because I am a place of rest. – I do not ask who drew desire and pain from my heart and picked the tendrils of all my attributes. So I carry myself there lightly; and fall back relieved and newborn into the world. Here I stay! On the beach of exuberant contentedness. – When my mother died, the moon shattered. Once more he, the Lord, separated the water from the land. There is lightning! The glowing zigzag writes fiery words on the dark silk of the heavenly picture-book, a warning sign on the western wall of the world. God is rolling through the world!! His red initial struck me and inspired me before it was extinguished in the sea. – Do you still remember the time we were at the loving seashore at midnight? I refused to sail out with you upon the flowing jewelry that late at night. The astrologer had given me a stern warning about the black-lit hour between night and the night of Uranus. We, however, sailed forgotten through the eternal flood of love. "Tooh!" That is the foghorn . . . "Tooh!!" As the meadowlark calls over the grain-fields, again and again one hears the worried yellow sound over the trickling dark wheat of the sea. Rolling with the great water, we had become enmeshed in the fog. When it cleared, you hurried on into the world; but I remained on the dock and took delight in the fresh hybrid flower of the foaming green ocean. Never did its water smell so tangy as in the very early morning. Mussel and salt and alga and starfish combine, and the fish contributes the mother-of-pearl of his scales to the new wine.

> Curious people gather at the beach and presumptuously
>   compare
> Themselves with the sea and with me, the poet.
> But their empty words are erased by the sand.
> Faced with the world, I have forgotten the world,
> Watered by the noble dampness of the sea
> As if I lay in the wide hand of God.

THE GINGER CAT

My father knew how to skip school better than any other schoolboy. His tossed, down-filled quilt covered the floor with a snow of feathers. And time and time again my strict grandfather believed that the young rascal was on his way to school. He, however, lay stretched out between the thick red- and yellow-striped mattresses with the ginger cat in his arms. My amusing father can unfortunately no longer tell his favorite story about Aunt Jettchen. That was the name of his *ginger cat*. This story in particular is the one he used to tell us children in his inimitably vivacious way. We had to hold on to the backs of our chairs in the storm of his words.

His heart was never calm, which is precisely why he avoided the dull lessons at school. He was little concerned with anything that did not want to grow up wildly with him, that did not come flying into his mouth or his two ears. The ABC lay in his *mooka* or cubbyhole one evening, baked from sweet dough. All of a sudden, he could read and write. *Mooka* was the name he and his twenty-two sisters and brothers had for the hiding-place in which each of the children kept his or her apples and pears and nuts and sweets. – My father couldn't do arithmetic even in his later years – which is probably why no one in the city ever seriously called him to account. The system of telling time remained a mystery to him until his death. He always blamed poor Aunt Jettchen, saying she had kept him from doing everything. Only not from stupid tricks, these he still liked to play on us children. So no one ever considered him an adult. And his exceptional talent for organization made him seem like a child prodigy. The marks that my twelve-year-old papa brought home from the school in the village of Hexengäsecke were always the occasion for new outbursts of rage. "I'll put him in the reformatory!" Then the ginger cat's eyes became horrifying and she sprang at Grandpapa's face. In the meantime, my father escaped, tramped over the young lawns outside and nibbled on unripe fruit from the fruit trees. Then his good mother would later secretly call him into the house; compensating for the slap in the face that his father had given him with an even richer honey-cake heart. She always had various hearts or cookies made of macaroon dough lying ready on a porcelain bowl with little cupids for just such occasions. He and his ginger cat then took off contentedly, springing over the green animal hedges of Westfalia. And finally he cut the tails off the ducks and geese made of pink and white hawthorn leaves, and wherever he still saw a window open, he would throw such a curiosity "into the parlor." But he courteously brought his own mother a bouquet he had picked himself of colorful immortelles; to touch the raisin of her soft ring-cake heart. Yes, she was powerfully moved. Arthur Aronymus was her favorite of her twenty-three children. Even if he did come tearing into the carpeted room with muddy shoes – "he is still the best of them all!" she reassured the infuriated Grandpapa. Finally my father, who was also moved, took a honey heart from the cupid bowl for himself and pinched a little one for Aunt Jettchen. Purring, she brought both hearts, as trained, into Arthur's *mooka* in the wall by his bed. Until late at night the two of them were up happily eating the honeyed remnants of the day.

At first, my father could not endure the ginger cat, couldn't stand Aunt Jettchen. She had to suffer many a knock and kick from him. And how often he frightened her with his cork gun. But one day, overpowered by her cat charms, he made friends with her, the bright animal. At bedtime, Aunt Jettchen simply came leaping from the yard into his bedroom; first she had to hear the three older brothers, who shared the room with my father, snoring heavily. Because she had stopped walking stealthily; her silent steps annoyed my father and he showed her every day how she was to walk. After lunch he routinely awakened his father, who had just fallen asleep under the thousand-year-old beech tree. Then his brothers would attack their inconsiderate brother and give him a good hiding. They were still finding fault with him when we, his children, were already grown up. He spoke too overpoweringly for them, as with many tongues, like an entire choir. Even when he was a little good-for-nothing, his mama could hear him coming from the end of the village. That was where the schoolhouse was, which is why she always knew whether he had skipped school or attended. But Aunt Jettchen used to be the best informed. Because she brought her friend as far as the big school gate and waited for him behind a petroleum barrel belonging to a spice store. Arthur used to buy himself gumdrops there for the way home. She so liked to watch him pull them out of his mouth in long strings and pop them back in again, and she rubbed her ginger fur affectionately against his checked pant-legs. Then my little papa knew that she was laughing with pleasure the way cats do. But Grandfather continuously kept a serious eye on him. He used to get the names of the other sisters and brothers confused or even tell the youngest of his sons and daughters to get out of the big garden, until they shyly called out from in front of the fence: "But we're your children." – How I would like to live in Paderborn . . . my little papa imagined to himself. There he would even go to high school regularly. He wished that he too would be thrown out by mistake as were the youngest children and the howling twins, so that he could, with a good conscience, run off with the foreign tradesmen who now and then traveled through the Westfalian villages peddling their wares, offering the girls jewelry, silks and little embroidered slippers and velvet ribbons with gleaming bangles, hair nets, necklaces, bracelets, and capes. With the gypsies, who had set up their tent a little while ago on the gentle rise between the ruined walls of the medieval tribunal, with them Arthur would have liked to disappear some day like the poor walled-in witches. His shocked mother's brown velvet eyes were full of water when her wild darling told her that. She reproached my grandfather for his unfair way of raising children. Every evening Aunt Jettchen licked my poor papa's tear-flooded face. He began to treasure her more and more. The big *mooka* was soon emptied out. Of course the presents had to be eaten inaudibly, and when the rock candy crunched between the boy's broad teeth, the ginger cat would cast a warning glance at my father. On many occasions the gentle comforter returned his hospitality with a fat young mouse, which she served her true friend, my father, in bed. Those were the only times that my father went to school. It was great fun for him to furtively slip the bloody catch into the teacher's coat pocket.

Aunt Jettchen! That is what everyone in my grandparents' house called the ginger cat, even my strict grandfather himself used to call the good animal: Aunt Jettchen!! Basically, he was touched by her devotion to his good-for-nothing. All the twenty-three siblings called the ginger cat: Aunt Jettchen; the maids in the house, the farmhands on the big estate, the milk-maids in the stable; the cows and the spotted oxen, the donkey, the peacocks in the garden, the chubby-cheeked naked angel in the fountain, the lambs in the meadow and their shepherd; but also the spitz, Aung Jettchen had great respect for him. All the schoolchildren asked about Aunt Jettchen, indeed, all the inhabitants of Hexengäsecke loved her. But she made a show of nobility in her choice of company and in her gestures! In general, she surrounded herself with an embonpoint like the oldest female member of a long-standing family. Why did she feel this preference for the unbridled wild creature, of all people? No one in the entire family could grasp that with any human understanding, except for the mother. Yes, the lovable animal got more accustomed to little Arthur every day and liked him better and better by the hour. She forgave him, miaowing, when he turned her around herself like a top by her ringed tail. Woe betide any of his brothers who insulted Aunt Jettchen! He noticed that right away, she got a migraine then – and lay on one of the branches in front of the window from which Arthur's sisters loved to watch the sunset. Dora and Lenchen were so sympathetic, Elise buried herself deep in her novels, and Fanny, the eldest, practiced playing the spinet. When she sang: "In a cool valley a mill-wheel turns, . . ." and my naughty papa suspected that she was about to do so, he climbed onto one of the arabesques of the old manor house and made a clatter like the wheelworks of the mill. And Aunt Jettchen's melancholy miaowing would keep time with his clattering; especially when a suitor stood at the spinet and was just beginning to caress Fanny's little hands. Tears of rage at the rascal would still be shimmering in her long silk lashes hours later.

Once the porter of the small village school brought a quite large yellow letter with a seal on it to my grandparents' house. One could tell the content was portentous just by the look of it. Grandfather read: To the noble and highly regarded fellow citizen M. Schüler of Gäsecke in Westfalia, because his fourteen-year-old son Arthur Aronymous is not attending school. The message stuck in the stunned patriarch's throat. But then it fell like hail from the cool, arrogant lips onto my little father. At this point, when he told us about it, we all cried together with him. That was actually the beginning of the tragic epoch of his life. He couldn't get proper sleep anymore. His father watched with eagle eyes to make sure he went to school. The maid shook him awake at six o'clock in the morning, chased the cat out of his arms without a thought for its feelings, and checked to see that Arthur also washed the two madcaps, his eyes. But Aunt Jettchen had taught him that long ago, she who washed her fur several times a day. She purred at him soothingly, and from that time forth she liked to steal the maid's smoked herring from her plate. But my father suddenly made up his mind again to let school be school. It was still half dark, and his brothers were sleeping in their beds against the four walls, when he played them a prank in the true sense of the word with drum and trumpet. Still half dreaming, the brothers thought they were in a triumphant procession and whistled and yelled so loudly and for so long that their father came into their bedroom in his long nightshirt with his pointed nightcap on his head. His bright blue eyes looked at each of the awakened brothers like a cold sky. Only on the slumbering, innocent Arthur did his recognition rest for the first time with goodwill. But when the father had left the room, Arthur crept, with his Aunt Jettchen, between the padded walls to skip going to boring school. He excused himself later to his father, who himself had been witness to the deafening noise, by saying that he hadn't been able to fall asleep anymore at all and had sat down before school began on the damson plum tree in the schoolyard. The father was also convinced by carrying out his own inspection. On velvet slippers, he sneaked into the bedroom once again in the early morning, as Aunt Jettchen had done in former times when she was still too distinguished. He was visibly satisfied, though, when he saw the wide-awake, crumpled pillow on the floor beside my young father's bed. As he was about to leave the room, however, he was horrified to see Arthur's plush green schoolbag hanging by the door! . . . Aunt Jettchen, however, who was rolled up like a sausage, peeping out from between the mattresses, assessed the situation, sprang in a high arc out of the bed, grabbed the dangling schoolbag and was gone out the wide-open window in no time! "Even if he isn't skipping school anymore, it seems, he has to forget his schoolbooks," muttered Grandpapa and went back across the hall to Grandmama, making the gentle woman smile as he praised the intelligence of Aunt Jettchen, Arthur's devoted friend. And that evening at the pub, the regulars, fellow citizens of Gäsecke, presided over by my father's strict but moved father, discussed the wiles of the ginger cat.

WHEN THE TREES SAW ME AGAIN

I came from the sea. When the trees saw me again, a gentle movement of air lifted their branches to greet me. Wind and storm make it possible for tall and short trees, shrubs and bushes, all herbs and the most delicate flower stems to move as they wish. The atmosphere enables the plant to express itself; indeed it develops by mixing the essence of its temperament with the element of air, with its movements in nature, a gentle breeze or a storm with lightning and thunder. Just as the will of man is moved to actions that are pleasing to God by the acknowledgment of God. The more a tree is aglow with the desire to express itself, the more powerfully the air arms itself for a storm. The burning storms that are experienced in the desert are caused by the still-extant strong primal passions of the ancient Asian trees of the East. But the late murmuring of melancholy also wafts effortlessly from the tired, gentle blowing of the palms. And you should know, if you lie down under the willow, that its long branches, hairy with leaves, sing the song of anxious longing with the air from afar. Don't annoy the dreaming juniper tree or the mountain ash tree! Protect the birds' nests in their cool, hospitable arms.

Because the trees cause each bird's-egg to dream
And their blossoms come chirping out of the embryo.

In the end, I beg of you not to insult the pine-needle tree that I so admire, she, the Indian princess of all trees! The Godhead herself dipped her feathered dress in the emerald of the woods.

Basically, the plants express themselves in their plant kingdom the same way we humans do in our human kingdom, by procedures that are related to ours but unknown to us. *This* natural history lesson is taught by the green paperback picture-book of the world. It often lies in my lap, and I open it ceremoniously. That is how I know that we sin against the plant, namely against its flower; it is the soul of every leafy creation that, I convince myself again and again in late summer, wraps itself up in the body of the fruit; and fragrantly penetrates the peach and the robust apple. Since I convinced myself of this sweet wisdom, I only eat the body of the plant soul with great reverence. The black and the golden berries of the grape look at me. – The potential for expression of the trees and their tendrils influences the weather, whose changes we are accustomed to attributing to mathematical and astronomical laws. Why do we like to look so far afield; and everything is happening right in our midst? The tall, leafy, venerable giants rustle in our ears every day. Since the monstrous bloodquake that devoured all love, spattered the original Commandment with blood, extinguished the last glimmer of light. Even the protective, age-old Pride of India trees have to believe in this irrecoverable loss. How much more terrible it is, though, for the childlike meadows of lady's-smock, the carpets of forget-me-nots, and the slopes full of unsophisticated clover and yarrow. There can be no more real summer, no proper winter in the lands of hostility. Forests were sacrificed like a head, but it screamed to heaven. And yet how willingly the birch let itself be felled for my table at which I write; for your canopy, under which you dream of me. – The heated exchange in the plant kingdom was proven to us by the sickly heat of the days this past summer, which by no means bathed us in gold, in whose sun not even the coco grew, but in whose fever we scorched to a new death. And again, how little the winters resemble the winters of the snowmen over whose backs we used to slide on the way home from school. These are the results of the indifferent position that the trees, bare of their leaves, grew accustomed to taking toward the irreconcilable world. And *how* they loved their winter ermine! Dexterous branches shook down the first snow-stars for themselves from the gray bush of the winter cloud. So we have ruined things for ourselves with nature, with the merry green leaf people who give us ozone and the breath of life. The unpredictability of all-too-hot to all-too-cold is the result of the complaint of the plant world, which is turned completely upside down. We have lethally confused and wounded it. Because nature is not the footstool of mankind that we can push around or even saw through as we wish. The moon once put a spell on my branches; I dreamed early in the morning that I was a tree. And I understand why the flowers today, who never suspect anything evil, will turn their faces to the side in the splendor of their color, or why the young oak will hang her green curly head. Then we will die of thirst from the tepidness of the air, and our hearts will become old and suffocate. The restful mood of nature and her peaceableness create the true picture, the original of Creation. That is not to say that the tree should not rustle to its leaves' content or that the wave, its friend, should not surge up. Each work of art, whether it is a poem, a painting, or a song, infuses dull surfaces with the depth of a real creation. The cabala speaks of the "all-pervasive deity." The air currents receive their character from the plants and vice versa. We could still live in paradise today if we people were in agreement with each other.

TWO NONSENSE POEMS

People have advised me not to include the two dear poems
in the book. But I always ask the stars, and
now I am asking the reader.

I. THE POTATO PANCAKE

On the border between the Rhineland and Belgium it is called: Le Latka.

> Kaiser Karl in Aachen
> Liked to sit on the throne
> When he ate Le Latka
> With strong coffee.

For both peoples, the Germans and the Belgians, it is a favorite dish. The delicacy swims farther up the Rhine to the Swiss border.

> In Zürich, the vegetarian herdsman
> Actually comes from Bavaria.
> If your stomach feels queasy,
> It's because his cake swims in eggs.

In Cologne, Ohligs, Düsseldorf, Neuß, Hamm, Dortmund, Coblenz, and Neuwied the national dish has an almost electrical effect. Especially in Wuppertal, where the pancake's pan was, and in Elberfeld Barmen, where butter first came into the world. Originally it was fried in *pure* butter; today not entirely without butter even in the poorest sections of the Wuppertal cities. Half and half, however, is an insult to the tongue of the Wuppertal gourmet. – The cook peels large potatoes and grates them into batter. No flour is added, as it is in the Spree cuisine, but several whisked eggs, freshly laid Easter eggs. I almost forgot salt! To think that one cannot break the Berliners of the habit of baking the most sought-after dish of all dishes in kidney-fat or even lard.

> Oh, and above all in Dresden and Leipzig,
> Where the potato grates itself
> In the machine into pancake batter.

"Potato pancake" is what the North German calls our *dear* Latka.
> And what can happen in the end
> Is that one looks forward even during the day
>   to this magical dish.
> – It depends, of course, on the hometown of your cook
> – One can bite down on onions in the family pancake circle.

Eat potato pancakes! Especially as they are prepared in their fatherland, where they are among the most easily digestible dishes.

And not dishonored by pork;
Crisped in lard, the poor pig!
Yes, that is how the pancake is served in Berlin
Often in the most discriminating circles!

And the most outrageous thing is –

On top of that
They sprinkle it with sugar!
THE BERLINERS WILL LIVE TO REGRET THAT!

It is precisely the slight sharpness of its taste, as it is prepared in Wuppertal, that provides never-dreamed-of, browned illusions for the palate.
Eat potato pancakes!!!!
I don't withstand the temptation either, and let myself be tempted by it.
Lottchen (rapturously): "In sweet cream onion butter, man, it is – a poem" . . .
Even a classical one:

Who is crunching so late through the night and the wind?
It is a potato pancake in Auntie's locker.*

Incidentally:

It is written in capital letters in the stars,
That the inhabitants of the moon love potato pancakes;
And bake them almost every Sunday.
Just ask Einstein, he is often their guest.

*This is an imitation of the "Erlkönig" or "King of the Elves," a poem by Goethe, made famous by Schubert's musical setting:
Who is riding so late through the night and the wind?
It is the father with his child.
Wind, Kind [child], and Spind [locker] rhyme.

Since even Lucullus was eating them with enthusiasm,
His cook, who was otherwise in a terrible rage,
Baked potato pancakes without grumbling.

The Shah of Persia, Abdullah,
Found a woman's blond hair in the pancake.
– He had the woman come to him . . .

Even Bonaparte ate them,
Latkas with Josephine.
Whether Werner Krauß Napoleon
– Likes them? I think so.

And further, freely according to Schiller's text,
Until I have pancakes coming out my ears –
I could turn armies of them out of the frying pan,
They would all be served steaming hot.

I dedicate the first to dear Hedwig Wangel:
Hedwig Wangel bakes the cake piously in vegetable oil
And spices the batter with her love, strong salt,
For her poor girls' choir of ex-convicts.
The cake is wolfed down at the gate of hope.

Please, write a pancake rhyme yourselves! – Well then:

> We sit, Dear Poet, like a duet
> At your place in the Saxon Inn, at the doll's stove,
> This earth is turning into paradise –
> But our cake is hard as – a – board.

2. THE HEAD COLD

I have it again! Sneezing has become unfashionable.

> In the Biedermeier years,
> When people were still warmhearted,

Both husband and wife said "Bless you!" to each other
Or "To your health! if I may be permitted."

But in the course of the decades most people, with no pangs of
conscience, have forfeited the pleasantries of social graces and
no longer say anything to extol sneezing. They are ready with
prescriptions.

I still wear my sneeze with dignity
And don't blame it on the unpredictable summer weather.
Somehow, I find "complaining" absurd,
When one can still breathe a bit.
If only a publisher would relieve me of my burden,
Which hangs unpublished from my boughs.
The many verses only then become a jewel
When a publishing house urges that they be ready to print.
Poems that I scrawled in recent years,
Light pink prose, odds and ends, for what they're worth –
I laced the world into it en passant,
Providing evidence that I know how to write.
And would really be able to write by return mail poste re-
    stante.
Why are you rushing to relieve my cold,
As if we were almost blood relations.
– At night I put a dab of cotton wool in my nose –
Previously dipped in glycerine – and then I snore.

THE SHINING TREE

It was like a person to me, so dear – and still is today. It doesn't
have glowing cheeks anymore, and has turned yellow, extremely yellow. Even last month there were still pomegranates hanging from it, and its delicate leaves were the purest

blossoming green ruffled lace. How quickly it wasted away! Together with me, it got annoyed about the intolerable crowing of the roosters at a tactlessly early hour, because it was a short, noble, chivalrous tree, I think it was a marquis. How often I heard it exclaim "mais donc" when the rooster with his waddling women came walking directly under its noble branches hung with blood. In the yards of the summerhouses, low walls separate rooster from rooster. Goats bleat too, but that seemed to rather amuse my shining tree, judging by the movement of its branches. I don't like to look through my window at the garden courtyard anymore. Not even the two girlfriends of my noble tree are there anymore. Granted, their skeletons still exist, two ghosts, on whose withered arms the unsuspecting sparrows sit, waiting for their manna from heaven. Between the bare trees November is freezing, November the grave-digger, who is waiting for the third tree, "for my delicate tree." Its thin leaves get weaker and yellower by the day, and the last shriveled berries have fallen into the sparse grass below: pomegranates, drops of blood, love, farewell.

PRAYER

When someone prays fervently, his soul goes to the entrance of the body. If someone dies in prayer, the soul is spared the farewell, not only from its own body, but also the final farewell from the womb of the world. To emerge from that is: to die. And yet, according to heavenly laws, it is a matter of being born again. The mortal frame tears asunder, but the eternal bud of breath lives an eternal life, survives death forever. Because the source of *being born* springs from the creation of the world! The decaying, personal world of the body, which falls away, renounces its divine jewel that lives on, not the personal awareness of existence. But vice versa. The soul that leaves its body extinguishes all consciousness of its frame. Sleep, by way of contrast, deadens the body temporarily; and the soul of the creature is able to leave the body that has surrounded it all its life. The dream is the melted portrait of the soul that it left behind for its slumbering home while it was temporarily absent in search of divine adventure. So the darkness of sleep gives the soul the opportunity to get away, to go on holidays again and again. Bodies that remain awake prevent it from traveling. The soul, however, forcibly demands its rights. If it never comes back again, the body will decay. But the forbidden path that combines heaven and earth has not been walked by anyone without the will of God, not even by a soul. – The person who halfheartedly and routinely says his prayers, who prays, in order to have prayed, will never get as far as a heart is wide, and will never encounter the angelic harbingers of eternity here on earth. To the prophets, prayer was the highest ceremony; the miracles of heaven that they encountered made them into saints. Everything that can be proven is preceded by something that cannot, and vice versa. But woe to the hungry heart that is fed by the miserly chef of a limited understanding. In the original plan of Creation, each thing in the world moves with the revolving original thesis of the hand of the clock to the call of the original cuckoo of the universe. But an ear that is not listening to the world ticktock of the methodical world comes either too early or too late.

God always knows what time it is. To meet your man Friday, who will pray together with you, and will dig between the streets of time in the jungles of eternity, is the good fortune of a God-seeking person. To hit on divine expression, together with Friday, is the crowning goal of the courageous, religious Robinson Crusoe–style adventure. Our earth, like all the earths that we unfortunately can see only as tantalizing, far-off, fire-guarded visions, is of the body, as we creatures are, a finite piece of infinity. Eternity clamped in time.

It is to this system in the creation of the eternal that we owe our thanks for the *existence* of our world, thanks mixed with sadness about the loss of our inspired, paradisal world. Picked fresh from eternity, shining in blossom, it was called: paradise. I have already written elsewhere that I consider the body of the world and the bodies of the creatures, indeed everything physical, to be an illusion of the soul, a crystallization of the soul that longs to go home to safety and security in the hand of God the Father. Because every soul is an eternity and, untied from the original eternity, yearns to enfold itself in the shelter of a frame. The soul of an animal, by way of contrast, somehow still blindly hangs on to the cosmos in its illusion of a body, not yet consigned to earthly responsibility. The poet, when writing, has an enhanced awareness of the half-slumbering animal state, which is also the state of plants and stones. Creative writing is like being beside God. How else could the chosen ones who are possessed by the urge to write take upon themselves the inhuman responsibility of wisdom? The prophet, oldest brother of the poet, inherited the cultivation of the conscience directly from the Creator. The cultivation of the conscience, though, also ennobles the poet, and the slightest step from the path takes its revenge, naturally, on the credibility of his verse. So poetry happens, and is written down by the chosen poet: the extract of higher truth. Writing poetry is a grace that the poet accepts. And even the poem that quarrels with God kneels before him. The poet knows well that it takes a lifetime of absorption in one's work and previous lives of such absorption before he finds even a single "glowing word of love" between the expanses of the world, a word that will temporarily release his soul from the star while he is still on earth. But this miracle of inspiration wafts over every human heart, the storm of love over its blood, and drives the rest of its original blood's gold up from the depths onto the beach. Original blood is gold that has been kept, that conjures up a state of happiness when it encounters the original blood of the loving person. Original blood upon original blood results in: paradise. Glowing and causing the other to glow, only people exhilarated by love can recognize each other. – I watch the big birds – they cannot tell us stories from the green, eternal picture-book, between whose leaves they hover; but their song makes the blossoms awake on the branches and the shoots want to sprout. That is how humans perceive animals, since they somehow still have one of their poles resting in the original world with all their desires and passions. We never entirely understand them. The rest remains a secret!

Because humans are detached from the cosmos, from the outline of the original world in the environment: the prison of time. The human lives in time, the animal in nature, and the soul of the plant in its integrated green illusion of a leaf. How often it happens that when a type of tree dies in the farthest east, at the same time the same kind of tree begins to wilt at the opposite end of the earth. That bears witness as to how the plants are interconnected through their sap, a connection that winds itself through hedge after hedge. Only seldom does a person suspect the situation of the person next to him, at least clairvoyance does not force him to decay at the same time. More so the animal; it lives in the vegetation, the human in the atmosphere. The Creator duplicated plants and animals thousands of time in the plan of Creation. Once the human was created, however, and placed in the glowing Eden of the world, he divided him into two halves. And so the human always feels compelled to divide himself in order to find himself again.

I wish a terrible pain would make itself felt
And I would fall to the ground
And suddenly be torn toward myself.

So it came about that people finally split into nations, separated humans who reunite in love in accordance with the book of Creation.

The land and the oceans live in harmony side by side
Why is it that human beings break from humanity
And have to collect themselves again in higher events?

Only a creature that is *delivered* from the colossus of material is divisible. Mankind cannot avoid having to account for himself before God. Animals, still partially unborn in blind primal consciousness, behave without responsibility. That is why the human, on account of his entire separation, is the most perfect of God's creations, but consequently also mentally and geographically the farthest removed from the ways of God; however, with the overview of perspective, he can conquer the heavenly sphere for himself in its entirety. The animal, like the plant, and also the stone, still clinging to a certain extent to the string of Creation, belong to the works not yet carried to full term between the divine and earthly spheres. Our world shone on God's globe in the original light. And only its darkening gave birth to sin, the result of great confusions. So it is illogical to make the "sinner" responsible for his sin – the prophets, in particular, looked after "those who lost their way."

Paradise became the earth, but our thoughts and actions, which have become blind, move in the footprints of a thousand centuries of the world. The cabala teaches of the "all-pervasive deity." Only God alone possesses the strength to guide the course of the world, in tranquility and in stormy times. Think of the stormy landscapes of great artists, kept in a methodical outline. In fact, that determines the artistic value of the paintings! The complete separation of man from eternity, paralleled in the universe, differentiates between him and the animal and the plant and the stone and makes him master of the world. The heathen's idolization of the animal rests on the animal's mystification. This mixture of the knowable and the unknowable is what kindles animal-*worship*. Still babbling like a child, the belief of these original people plays with creating fear. Think of the sphinx and of the mysterious idol with the bird's head: Osiris. Old and strong, the people of Jehovah, of the invisible, one God, differed from all the other peoples in their religion based on the invisible hereafter. The idols are a horror to the God who said: "I AM WHAT I AM."* In the ecstasy of writing, every poet probably becomes a heathen at some time – even I did, when I wrote my poem "Jacob":

> Jacob was the buffalo of his herd,
> When he stamped his hooves,
> The earth flashed fire under him.

> Bellowing, he left his piebald brothers,
> Ran into the primeval jungle, to the rivers,
> Staunched the blood there of his monkey bites.

> The tired pains in his ankles made him
> Sink down in a fever before heaven.
> – And his ox-face invented the smile.

The poem has its most powerful effect on natural readers or listeners. But also on Egyptologists. The idol brings things about, God wants to reign. It is written in the cabala . . . "When the bull smiles, the lamb will be born." This revelation took me by force in verse. There is no question of vanity here, and I affirm that, before writing my Hebrew ballad "Jacob," I never

*A translation of the origin of the word "Jehovah."

160

in my life read in the cabala or knew of its content through hearsay. I bow humbly before my sacred inspiration. – The animal and the plant, will they ever be separated from eternity and, fully conscious of it, lead a life among us people? The great painter of the animal saints, the Blue Rider, the Messiah of the animals, Franz Marc, loved the animals *so much* that he became knowing of them; and spoke of the pure manner of death when the tiger fetches the gazelle for itself from the cliff. The animal kills out of uncomplicated hunger, the human kills the human. The animal's impulse, still unadulterated, but also having no sense of consideration, still rolls the colossus of the world, together with the elements of creation. Awareness of the animal is the desire to tame it, as paradoxical as that may sound, a tasteless outrage. One should not attempt to meddle with the animal's elemental world slumber between time and eternity. Such attempts always remain painful, piti-ful premature births, disruptive interferences in the will of the Creator. Don't train them! BUT BE GOOD TO THE ANIMALS!! God is their witness.

God moves in repose through the world, God is the signpost and the threshold. We always have to go by way of him, and the movement in people moves according to the moving of the Creator. The deviant person, who walks along unevenly in the beat of the universe, is mistaken in the system of cre-ation and loses his balance. Every disruption in the universe is a result of lagging behind or racing ahead of the beat of God. A disturbance of one's sense of balance is the result of the event that deviates from the method of the world. May the exemplary tempo, with which people should comply from the moment of their birth, move humanity again! To gain this tempo, one should become absorbed in God, in this – policy of eternity. Life means prosperity. Above all in the wheat of the soul, but also in the common property of the fruit and the bread. Because every creature was held in a motherly womb that placed the body to which it gave birth *trustingly* in the world womb of all mothers. The earthly life consists of three cases that we must break through in order to be free again and come to God. Thus, our life takes place doubly encased in temporal wombs of eternity. Still enclosed and protected in the most extreme physical illusion of the world: earthly existence takes place invisibly. And yet we people are God's *free* offspring. Each true prayer is a concentration . . . I and I. And out of this combination with oneself comes double the strength. Indeed, the prophets pulled at God! when they thundered the truths into the hearts of the people. And so often divinely exuded the sacred clause in countless verses. God's powerful falcons came screaming upon him and experienced already in the illusion of their body the echo of imprisoned eternity, God the unsurroundable. I would like to give the reader a quiet hour with my prayer, into which I put a rare flower now and then, as into a festoon. Its fragrance should not intoxicate him, but awaken him. To be awake brings conscience after it. God is *the one who is awake!* We people, however, mutually bury our conscience to the point of degeneration, and yet we possess that jewel of the most multifarious, clearest possibility of consciousness. God is a "deity of all repose." All passions rest in his holy siesta.

Other Volumes in the European Women Writers Series: